A
CONFUSION
OF
TIME

A
CONFUSION
OF
TIME

COLIN WOOD

Thomas Nelson Inc., Publishers
NASHVILLE   NEW YORK

Copyright © 1975 by Colin Wood

All rights reserved under International and Pan-American Conven-
tions. Published by Thomas Nelson Inc., Publishers, Nashville, Ten-
nessee. Manufactured in the United States of America.

First U.S. edition

Library of Congress Cataloging in Publication Data

Wood, Colin.
  A confusion of time.

  First published in England under title: The Alabama story.
  SUMMARY: Confined to his bed in an old London house, a boy
journeys back in time to the nineteenth century where he becomes
involved with the lives of his home's former inhabitants.
  [1. Space and time—Fiction] 1. Title.
PZ7.W84733Co   1977   [Fic]   77-12477
ISBN 0-8407-6553-3

To
Liz, Mary, Nick, Tim, and Paddy
and in memory of
Frances

CONTENTS

A
CONFUSION
OF
TIME

1

UPSTAIRS, DOWNSTAIRS

in which Master Raymond Price (downstairs) meets Miss Laura Hamilton (upstairs) and becomes involved in a somewhat topsy-turvy situation not unconnected with a midget-sized man, a giant-sized dog, and a plump and portly cook.

Raymond lay in bed watching the legs and feet go by. All he could see of people was their legs and feet because he lived in a basement room and so the pavement was above the level of the window.

Legs and feet, legs and feet. All day long they went by. So many different shapes and sizes. Some trotted, some plodded, some hurried, some dawdled. Usually the children's trotted or dawdled, while the grown-ups' hurried or plodded. There were the dainty legs of young ladies with high-heeled shoes, the huge legs of workmen with hobnailed boots, the plump and motherly legs of middle-aged women with baskets bumping on each side of them, the long springy legs of young men with tight-fitting trousers and suede zipper boots. There were also crippled legs, bent legs, twisted legs, bandy legs—quite a lot of these, in fact, because Raymond lived in a mill town in the North, where often in times of poverty the millworkers' children had been so badly fed that their bones grew soft and curved instead of strong and straight. Raymond's mother was a millworker, and when she came home at night, she often told him about the hard times that her parents and grandparents had suffered in the old days.

9

Just now, however, Raymond wasn't thinking about the old days—he was thinking about today and how to while away the long hours until his mother came back from work. It was still only nine o'clock, and she wouldn't be home till half past six. He had some new library books, a comic or two, and, of course, his railway annuals, but he was already tired of reading. And he had a new jigsaw puzzle with over a thousand pieces in it, but today he felt a little more ill than usual and his back ached badly when he tried to twist himself around to the bedside table where he did his jigsaws.

Until a few weeks ago he had been allowed to get up a bit during the day to do some model making at his little workbench or play with his train layout in the corner of the room. But now the doctor said he must stay in bed all the time. How long the hours seemed! Of course Mrs. Nuttall would be coming in to give him his dinner and fluff his pillows up and talk to him a bit—that was something to look forward to. But what was to be done with the rest of the day? There wasn't even any television. A tube had blown in their battered old set, and his mother said that she couldn't afford to replace it. There was nothing to look at but those endless feet and legs. He was so tired of seeing people cut off at the middle. He wanted to see a *whole* person for a change.

Suddenly a whole person appeared. He had a man's face with a large drooping mustache, and his head was as big as a man's but his body was smaller than Raymond's, who was not quite ten years old and very small for his age. The midget was wearing a crumpled gray suit, a small camel-colored overcoat, and a brown Homburg hat tilted slightly forward and to one side. Slung on a colored braid from his left shoulder to his right hip was a bright silver trumpet, and slung on a piece of string from his right shoulder to his left hip was a khaki knapsack like the ones workmen use to carry their lunch in. Accompanying him was a large Irish wolfhound that was almost as tall as its master.

They stopped right outside Raymond's house, which was on a busy corner at the end of a row of large Victorian mansions. The little man took off his hat, revealing a head as bald as an egg, with a fringe of fluffy white hair all around the back and sides, sticking up like a halo. He bowed to his dog and offered him his hat, which the dog received between his teeth and held upside down like a basin. Then the dog stood up on his hind legs—he was certainly *much* taller than his master now—and the two did an old-fashioned waltz together. Finally the dog sat down, still with the hat between his teeth, and the little man lifted the trumpet to his lips and started to play a tune.

Raymond knew the tune—"When the Saints Go Marchin' In." He remembered, ages ago, when he had still been allowed to go to school, all the children had sung it over and over again at the tops of their voices coming home on the bus from the school outing to the seaside. He had been thrilled by that singing. But he was even more thrilled now by the way the midget played the tune on the trumpet. He had never realized before that a trumpet could make such a lovely sound, so pure and clear and smooth. The well-known tune, which had sounded so jolly on the coach trip, now sounded almost sad, but Raymond liked it better that way since he had noticed before that sad things are often somehow beautiful.

All the same, the little man was careful not to make it sound *too* sad. He kept putting extra bits into the tune which were not exactly funny but so clever and unexpected—and yet at the same time so expected—that they made Raymond feel like laughing deep down inside. He felt as if he could go on listening to that trumpet for ever, without ever getting bored or anything.

While the tune was being played, the dog walked up and down on its hind legs, collecting money in the hat from passersby. Raymond couldn't tell how much was being collected, but it must have been enough to satisfy the midget because after a while he stopped playing, called the dog over, emptied the money into his knapsack, and replaced the hat on his head. As he did so, he glanced down through the area railings and caught sight of Raymond's pale face staring up at him through the window. He grinned in a friendly way, did two or three steps of a little tap dance, raised his hat politely but comically like Charlie Chaplin, and started to walk down the area steps to the basement door.

Before Raymond had time to realize what was happening, the door opened and the little man, complete with trumpet, knapsack, and dog, stood before him.

"Excuse me for intrudin'," said the small man, "but could you oblige me with a drop of hot water for my brew o' tea. It's thirsty work, the trumpet. And mebbe you could spare a bowl of cold water for Mullinger 'ere, if 'e asks you nicely."

Mullinger went up to Raymond's bed, wagging his tail so hard that he nearly lost his balance. He wrinkled his nose up until his top lip curled right back, revealing his white teeth in a foolish smile. Raymond, who had never seen a dog smile before, laughed out loud, whereupon Mullinger stood on his hind legs and looked very pleased with himself.

"Yes, you can make some tea. The kettle's there on the stove. And Mullinger can have as much water as he likes. There's a big bowl in that cupboard."

It seemed, though, as if the little man knew exactly where to look for everything. He had found the bowl almost before Raymond had stopped speaking, and he went straight behind the screen to the sink, even though Raymond had not told him where to look for the tap. In next to no time he had brewed up his tea in his rather chipped enamel mug and begun to sip it— rather noisily but with evident pleasure. In between sips he addressed himself to Raymond.

"Things 'ave changed a bit in this 'ere kitchen, 'aven't they? You see, I used to come 'ere to see my grandmother when I were a lad—that's nigh on fifty year ago. And she were fifty years in the service of old Mr. 'Amilton, the one who owned the biggest cotton mill around 'ere in days gone by. But perhaps I ought to introduce myself. 'Ere's my card."

Raymond took the small white card, on which, in elegantly printed letters, the following words appeared:

WALTER WILBERFORCE TULLIVER
CHIMNEY SWEEP, BUSKER, AND ESCAPE ARTIST
TEL. BLACKSTONE 123

Raymond was rather puzzled by the card. He knew what chimney sweeps were, of course, but he had never heard of buskers or escape artists. He wanted to ask for an explanation, but his mother had told him that it wasn't polite to ask too many questions of strangers. So he contented himself with saying:

"You don't look very much like a chimney sweep, Mr. Tulliver."

"Call me Wally—all me friends call me Wally—an' I 'hope I can count you as one of my friends?"

"Oh, yes, Mr. Tulliver—Wally, I mean. I'd like to be one of your friends. My name is—"

"Don't tell me! Let me guess." Wally took a big slurp of his tea and screwed up his eyes as if he were thinking very hard. "You certainly don't look as if you're called Archibald."

"No, I'm not."

"There you are," said Wally triumphantly. "I told you I'd guess."

"But you still don't know what I'm called."

"Ah, but I know what you're *not* called, and with a little 'elp from Mullinger 'ere we can soon find out what you *are* called. You don't mind if I enlist the 'elp of Mullinger, do you?"

"Of course not."

"Right, then. Mullinger, this 'ere boy 'as a name somewhere about 'im. Now you know that a person's name sticks to that person like a scent, an' 'e can't shake it off no matter what 'e does. I want you to sniff out this boy's name, Mullinger. Are you ready?"

Mullinger gave a wag and a nod. Wally closed his eyes again and began to recite:

"Adam, Alan, Harry, Dick,
Roger, William, Tom, Tim, Nick,
Patrick, Peter, James and John,
Basil, Bertram, Algernon,
Cyril, Cecil, Raymond . . . "

At the mention of "Raymond," Mullinger barked very loudly and stood on his hind legs. Wally patted him and chuckled delightedly.

"Raymond, eh? Well, Raymond, there's not much doubt about that, is there? Mullinger knows a lot of things. 'E knows when there's a tom cat two streets away, or a dog two miles away. He knows 'oo's happy and 'oo's sad, 'oo's wicked and 'oo's good. He knows when it's going to thunder, or when a plane's going to crash or a ship's goin' to sink. . . . "

"Can he really see into the future?"

"Course 'e can. The past as well. The future an' the past are all the same to 'im. For instance, this 'ere room—I remember it from years ago, but Mullinger, 'e can sniff wot was 'ere many years before I was born, back in Mr. 'Amilton's time, when Miss Laura 'Amilton were just a little girl, an' Lord Palmerston were Prime Minister, an' Queen Victoria not much older than our Queen is now. . . . "

As Wally was speaking, Mullinger began prowling around the room, uttering little whimpers of excitement. He kept going behind the screen and pawing at it, until it began to rock rather dangerously. Wally went over to it, and although he was so small, he folded it up with his strong little arms and laid it down on the floor.

Behind it, instead of the little sink and the tiny gas cooker, Raymond saw a big kitchen stretching right back through the house. There was a large plain wooden table in the center, at which a fat cook and a plump kitchen maid, both dressed in mobcaps and long skirts swathed in huge aprons, were cleaning and slicing vegetables in enormous earthenware bowls. A cheerful fire was burning in the kitchen range, and all the ovens had been polished with blacklead until they shone. On various smaller benches or tables around the kitchen, cooking implements were set out ready for use—a tray of wooden steak beaters, a set of potato mashers, a rack of glass rolling pins, and an apple peeler made of iron and wood resembling a miniature mangle. One whole side of the room was covered by a giant cupboard on which plates and dishes of every shape and size were displayed, and on another cupboard were arranged pans, cooking bowls, jelly molds, baking trays, and cake stands big enough to hold cakes that would feed an army. There was a bread cutter that looked like a guillotine, a coffee roaster that resembled a steam engine, and a kind of wooden wheel on iron legs that Raymond thought must be a knife cleaner. On the wall above a high mantelpiece hung a clock in a wooden case, a picture of the Duke of Wellington, and a large framed sampler on which were embroidered the following words:

Golden Rules for the Kitchen
Without Cleanliness and Punctuality, Good Cooking is
    impossible.
A Time for everything, and everything in Time.
A Good Cook wastes nothing.
An Hour lost in the Morning has to be run after all Day.
Haste without Hurry saves Worry, Fuss, and Flurry.
Stew boiled is Stew spoiled.
Wash vegetables in three Waters.

Raymond gazed in astonishment at this spectacle. Then, with a sudden terror, he saw the red-faced cook looking straight in his direction and heard her scream:

"Who let that boy into my kitchen?"

"I did, Cook," said a calm clear voice.

Turning around, Raymond noticed for the first time a little girl of about his own age, wearing a red velvet dress with white embroidered bib and cuffs, matching red ribbons in her pretty dark hair, and high white shoes cross-laced with red laces. She was standing behind him, as if she had slipped in from the side door.

"But, Miss Laura," said the cook, "you know very well that Master 'as strictly forbid the factory 'ands or their childer to come beggin' at the kitchen. There's plenty o' good bread an' gruel for them, as they well know, but they mun wait till it's sent over to t'coach 'ouse, an' not come troublin' us 'ere while we're preparin' it. An' look, miss," she wailed, as she suddenly caught sight of Wally and Mullinger, "look wot 'e's brought with 'im—a great big dirty dog and a . . . a . . . a dwarf!"

At the mention of the word "dog," Mullinger advanced toward her, smiling and wagging his tail, but, mistaking his smile for a snarl, she retreated hastily and seized the largest of the steak beaters.

"'E's barin' 'is teeth at me," she screamed hysterically. "I'll do 'im in, I will, if 'e attacks me!"

"He's only tryin' to be friendly, ma'am," said Wally, advancing in his turn; but he spoke too late, for Mullinger's waving tail had swept a jar of pickled onions off a low shelf.

With a shout of rage the cook charged at him, brandishing the steak beater, but as she charged she slipped on a large and juicy pickled onion, upset a small table laden with vegetables, and ended up sprawling on the floor, with turnips and cabbages thudding down all around her. Mullinger, who thought it was all a joke, started barking joyfully, the kitchen maid screamed and fainted, and Raymond looked around in panic for some way of escape. As he was just about to make a dash for the door that led up the area steps into the street, he felt his hot nervous fingers seized by a small cool hand, and he was dragged through a different door and up two flights of stairs, till he emerged on a spacious landing on the first floor of the house.

"In here, quick!" a voice commanded, and he found himself, breathless and still holding hands with Laura, in a charming little room which he knew at once must be her nursery.

Everything in the room, from the huge rocking horse with straw-colored mane and flaring yellow nostrils to the marigold-patterned curtains and chair covers, was gay and bright and jolly. Every shelf and ledge was covered with little ornaments or trinkets that Laura had collected or made. There were curiously shaped beach stones painted in bright colors, cameos set in clusters of shells, bunches of artificial flowers in posy holders with glass or mother-of-pearl handles, strings of beads made from melon seeds, glass paperweights with birds or beasts or dancers or huntsmen molded inside them. And there were plenty of toys too—lots of dolls, a dolls' house taller than Raymond, with twenty rooms, each one perfectly furnished, dozens of clockwork animals and insects (none of them broken), a puppet theater with Punch and Judy puppets, and a Games Compendium containing every game you could think of, from tiddleywinks to chess (and not a single piece of any game was missing, because they were all put away neatly in their separate compartments). Raymond gazed openmouthed at this array of lovely things, and then looked timidly at Laura.

"Will your father be cross if he finds me here?"

"Of course he won't. He's the kindest father in the world."

"But the cook said . . . "

"Oh, never mind her, she's an old crosspatch—and anyway she thought you were one of the factory children who had come for bread and soup."

"Well, my mother does work in a factory—but I didn't come for bread and soup."

"Of course you didn't. You came to play with me. You're the boy from downstairs, aren't you?"

"How do you know about me?"

"Wally and Mullinger told me about you. I asked them to bring you."

"Are they *your* friends too?"

"They're *everybody's* friends—even Cook's, although she'll not believe it."

"What shall we play at?"

"We'll play at hospitals," said Laura decisively, "because I know you're a sick little boy, so you can be a British soldier wounded at Sebastopol, and I'll be Miss Nightingale looking after you and nursing you back to health. Miss Nightingale is a friend of my father's and she told me all about her work in the hospitals out there."

Raymond was certainly feeling rather tired after all the excitement, so he let Laura make him a bed on the comfortable window seat, and put little splints and bandages on his arms and legs, and bring him little trays of dinner which he pretended to enjoy and little glasses of medicine (it was water really) which he pretended to turn his nose up at.

While she fussed around with her trays and pills, dressed in a real nurse's cap which Miss Nightingale had brought from one of her new hospitals, he gazed dreamily down into the street below and thought how nice it was to see the top halves of people for a change. Most of the men wore tall hats and frock coats, and the ladies' crinolines were so wide that there was hardly room for two of them to pass each other on the narrow sidewalks. Horse-drawn carriages sped back and forth, and sometimes a brewer's dray thundered over the cobbles, its great carthorses looking magnificent with ribbons in their manes and brasses on their shiny leather harnesses. As the long summer day moved into evening and evening toward night, the lamplighter came along to light the gas lights, and an old man appeared around the corner ringing a handbell and pulling a little cart which carried the label:

JOSHUA BUTTERWORTH
CRUMPETS, MUFFINS, AND OATCAKES A SPECIALTY

Laura slipped away down to the street and returned five minutes later with a tray of tea and a plate of buttered crumpets oozing strawberry jam at every pore.

But while she was out, Raymond had fallen fast asleep.

2

ALARUMS AND EXCURSIONS

in which Laura loses her papa, Raymond loses Laura, Mrs. Porson loses her heart, and a ponderous policeman loses his chance.

When Raymond woke up, it was morning. An ugly gray light was filtering through the basement window. His eyes hurt, and his whole body was aching. Somebody was talking behind the screen. He called out, "Laura?"

His mother came across to him, followed by the doctor, who was wiping his hands on a clean towel. Mrs. Price looked pale and anxious, but she put on a brave smile as she came toward the bed. Dr. Reynolds put down the towel and picked up a syringe from a tray of instruments on the table.

"You've had a weary night, dear," said Mrs. Price, taking hold of Raymond's burning hand and brushing the damp hair back from his forehead. "Dr. Reynolds has had a look at you while you were asleep. He thinks you need a little injection to help you get over this bad patch, don't you, Doctor?"

"Indeed I do," said the doctor, "indeed I do! What's been going on here since I last saw you? You certainly are a funny little fellow, up one minute and down the next."

"I only went up to play with Laura. Wally showed me the way—and Mullinger."

The doctor looked questioningly at Mrs. Price.

"Has he really been . . . ?"

Mrs. Price shook her head quickly and winked at the doctor.

Raymond felt too tired to explain, though he noticed the wink.

"Ah, well," the doctor went on, as he cleaned a little patch on Raymond's arm in preparation for the injection, "I don't mind you playing with Laura and . . . er . . . Willy and Dillinger, so long as you get some rest as well. Now, just one—little—prick . . . and it's all over. That didn't hurt much, did it?"

"Yes," said Raymond.

Usually he would have been polite and said no, but he felt cross with the doctor for just *pretending* to believe him about Wally and Mullinger, and for getting their names wrong. Grown-ups never believed you *really,* and they only ever *half* listened to what you said.

When the doctor had gone, Mrs. Price came back and began to make Raymond more comfortable. She gave him a clean pillow-case, sponged him down with cool water, and changed his hot and crumpled pajamas for a nice freshly ironed pair. She brought him a glass of lemonade and put her arm around him for a while as he sipped it through a straw. After a few sips he said:

"Mummy, what's a busker?"

"Oh, it's a sort of—entertainer. They dance or sing or play an instrument in the streets. You see them in London mostly."

"What's an escape artist?"

"Goodness, *that* I don't know. Unless it's one of those men who keep escaping from prisons, like train robbers and such."

"Oh, no, he's not one of those. He's much too nice to be a train robber. And anyway he's much too small."

"Who is, dear?"

"Wally. He's the friend I mentioned to Dr. Reynolds, but he didn't believe me. It's true about him, though. He gave me his card with his full name on it, and his telephone number. I'll show you."

He felt in the pocket of his pajamas, but the card wasn't there. Then he remembered that he had changed them, so he asked his mother to bring the dirty pair over from the table where she had tossed them. She hesitated a moment and then brought them across. The card wasn't in that pocket either.

Raymond felt puzzled and disappointed. He *knew* that Laura and Wally and Mullinger were real, but now he had no way of proving it. He watched his mother tidy the room and get ready for work.

"Mrs. Nuttall will be in earlier today," she said. "She's promised to pop in more often until you get a bit better. You'll probably doze for a while now that you've had that injection, so don't be alarmed if you wake up and find her here. It's a pity you're alone in this big house now that all the other flats are empty, but Mrs. Nuttall isn't far away. In any case, the corporation says that our new flat will be ready soon. Then we'll move out too, and this ugly old street will be demolished. And good riddance to it, I say!"

"It must have been a nice street once, in the old days," said Raymond.

"Oh, it was—one of the poshest streets in Blackstone. This house wasn't divided up into nasty little flats in those days. The Hamiltons lived here. Mr. Hamilton was a friend of Lord Derby and Lord Shaftesbury and Florence Nightingale—and a friend to the working people too. He owned the biggest mill around here, but he wasn't a greedy grasper like a lot of the mill owners."

"No, I know," said Raymond. "He used to give the poor workers gruel from his own kitchen—but they weren't allowed to come begging at the door for it, though. They collected it at the coach house."

"Goodness gracious, whoever told you that?" said Mrs. Price. "But I daresay you're right, though. That must have been at the time of the Cotton Famine."

"What was the Cotton Famine?"

"Oh, I can't tell you just now, dear. And in any case I think it'd be a bit hard for you to understand the ins and outs of it. I'm not sure that I understand it myself—but I know my grandmother used to tell me that Mr. Hamilton was a good friend to the working folk in those times."

Mrs. Price gave Raymond a kiss and a final tidy-up, and

bustled off to work. After she'd gone, he lay there for a long time watching the early-morning feet go by the window. What a lot had happened since yesterday morning! And yet—had anything really happened at all? Perhaps Dr. Reynolds was right, and it had all been just make-believe. With a heavy heart, Raymond turned on his side and pulled the covers up over his head. As he did so, something fluttered down onto his face. It was Wally's card, which had fallen from his pocket and lodged in a fold of the bedclothes.

At the same moment, the clear note of a trumpet could be heard along the street.

A few moments later Wally and Mullinger entered the room. Wally was carrying a bunch of flowers, and Mullinger was rather sheepishly wearing fancy ribbons on his tail and around his neck. As he brewed up his tea, Wally began to explain these unusual features to Raymond.

"We might 'ave a bit 'o trouble with that cook again—she certainly were a bit of a Tartar—so we've come prepared, 'aven't we, Mullinger, owd lad?"

Mullinger nodded his head and wagged his tail so vigorously that all his ribbons fell off. Wally sighed and replaced them carefully.

"The trouble is, he's such a great lolloping *dollop* of a dog. That's what frightened the cook. In them days folk weren't too keen on these waggling types of dogs, especially in posh houses. They preferred Pekinese and French poodles and the like. Now I reckon that if we disguise Mullinger as a poodle that cook'll fall for him like a ton o'bricks."

"She certainly fell like a ton of bricks yesterday." Raymond laughed.

"Alas, too true," said Wally. "But this time she'll fall *in love* with 'im. All women 'ave a soft spot for poodles—and Mullinger can look mighty like a poodle when 'e tries."

Mullinger hung his head and scraped his nose bashfully with one paw, but when Wally said, "Come on now, don't be shy," he stuck his tail daintily in the air, pricked up his ears, arched his neck, and trotted around the room with little springy steps, yapping politely as he did so.

"That'll soften 'er 'ard 'eart," said Wally. "But just in case it don't, 'ow about these?"

He flourished his bunch of flowers. Raymond looked at them doubtfully. It was rather an odd bunch. There was a long straggly sweet pea, a very tiny primula, a bulging peony, and a rather tatty-looking daisy.

"Back in them days," said Wally, noticing Raymond's puzzled look, "every picture told a story, and every flower had a meanin'. Sweet peas meant 'My love is new,' primulas meant 'Tender thoughts,' peonies stood for 'Hidden passion,' and daisies—well, I've just forgotten what daisies meant, but it was somethin' just as soppy."

"But . . . " Raymond was still doubtful, "do you think she'll get the meanings?"

"Of course she will. All the ladies understand the language of flowers—and as soon as she sees these flowers, why, she'll be so flattered that she'll give us the run o' the kitchen."

Before Raymond could raise any more objections, Wally had begun to fold up the screen and once again the huge kitchen appeared, but this time the kitchen maids were busy at the far end, and the cook was in earnest conversation with the butler, who was sitting by the fire enjoying a second breakfast of grilled steak, pork sausages, mushrooms, and sweetbreads, with a rasher or two of smoked bacon and a pint mug of strong coffee. As Raymond and his companions stood hesitating on the threshold of the room, they heard the butler saying:

"Quite frankly, Mrs. Porson, I don't agree with it. I don't agree with it at all! A gentleman like Mr. Hamilton shouldn't be wasting his time and money giving food and clothing to the work people. It's not *his* fault that the mills are all having to close down. It's the fault of those Yankees, blockading the Southern ports to stop the cotton supplies being sent over here. Mind you, Mr. Hamilton is making matters worse for both himself and the workfolk by supporting the Yankees. He ought to support the Southerners in this war, like all the other mill owners do—because the sooner the Southerners break the blockade, the sooner there'll be cotton for the mills, jobs for the workers, and profits for the owners. If Mr. Hamilton goes on like this, he'll soon be starving himself—and so shall we!"

The butler paused to demolish a plump sausage, which he had been wagging at Mrs. Porson on the end of his fork. While his mouth was still full, she ventured to reply:

"But you've got to admit, Mr. Smarmlin', that Mr. 'Amilton 'as a kind 'eart. 'E feels sorry for the poor workin' folk—an' 'e feels sorry for them poor black folks too, that them Southerners keep as slaves to pick all their cotton."

"My dear Mrs. Porson," said the butler, harpooning a juicy sweetbread in readiness for the next mouthful, "there will always be rich men, and there will always be poor, there will always be masters and there will always be slaves. One may perhaps feel *sorry* for the poor, but one should never try to *help* them."

He mopped up his bacon fat with a nice crusty slice of fresh bread, drained his coffee, and wiped his large glossy mustache on a red-spotted handkerchief.

"That was a very tasty snack, ma'am, and I'm very much obliged to you for it."

He went out by the far door, and Wally stepped forward into the room. He made a gallant bow and presented Mrs. Porson with the bouquet.

"Sweets to the sweet, ma'am," he said, simpering a little. "I 'ope you'll accept these flowers as a little token of my respect and—er—my regret for yesterday's unfortunate incident."

Mrs. Porson looked at the flowers, then at Wally, then at the flowers again. Raymond thought he noticed a little blush spreading over her face, though with such a red-faced person a blush was difficult to make out. Before she could reply, Mullinger advanced, doing his mincing poodle walk.

"Well, I'll be blessed," said Mrs. Porson, "that there dog looks like a different animal. 'As 'e got a bit o' poodle in 'im by any chance?"

"Yes, ma'am," said Wally. "Oodles of poodle! In fact 'is great grandfather were an aristocratic French poodle—came over 'ere at the time o' the French Revolution, right, Mullinger?"

Mullinger started to give a throaty bark but managed just in time to turn it into a squeaky yap.

"Well, I'll be blessed," said Mrs. Porson again. "I guess I *were* a bit 'asty yesterday. Might I ask, Mr. . . . ?"

"Tulliver," said Wally, offering her his card. "Walter Wilber-force Tulliver. Friends call me Wally."

"Might I ask, Mr. Wally, 'oo is this young feller as comes along with you?"

"This is Master Raymond Price, a friend of Miss Laura's. We was wonderin', ma'am, if we might use your kitchen as a shortcut up to Miss Laura's nursery?"

"I don't see no reason why not," said the cook, with a fond glance at her bouquet. "But Miss Laura, she's in no fit state to see visitors at the moment. Why don't you sit down an' let me make you a bite to eat an' somethin' for this dear little dog, an' then I can tell you 'ow it all came about."

In less time than it takes to tell, Mrs. Porson had set before them half a chicken, a veal-and-ham pie, the remains of a potato salad, and a huge dish of custard. For Mullinger, however, she produced only a tiny dish of chicken scraps, remarking, "I know poodles 'as very dainty appetites, so I won't overface 'im." Mullinger demolished this offering with one disdainful lick and crept gloomily under the table, where Raymond continued to feed him surreptitiously with lumps of pie.

"The 'ole trouble is," said Mrs. Porson, settling down to shell peas while her visitors tucked into their meal, "the 'ole trouble is that Miss Laura 'as 'ad too many burdens to bear since 'er poor mama died. She's nobbut a little mite o' nine year old but she's 'ad to be the lady of the 'ouse. She's far too growed up for 'er years, allus worryin' about 'er papa an' tryin' to get 'im to look after 'imself properly. An' now 'e's gone and disappeared."

"Disappeared?" cried Raymond in alarm. "How do you mean?"

"All as we know," said the cook, "is that the master went out yesterday afternoon to attend a meetin' wi' some of the other mill owners, an' 'e didn't come 'ome for dinner an' didn't send no message or anythin'. But she's a brave little soul, so she waited an' waited an' then took dinner alone in t' big dining room just as if nothin' were wrong. But Mr. Smarmlin' ses she only picked an' pecked at 'er food, an' Miss Peach—she's the governess—ses she were up several times in t' night askin' if 'er papa 'ad come 'ome yet. This mornin' she wouldn't touch 'er breakfast, an'—'ere, where's Master Raymond off to?"

Raymond had jumped up from the table and darted up the little stairs that led to the landing. The cook's words had filled him with alarm. Laura's papa was in some sort of trouble! He had to go and help her! When he got to the landing, his heart was thumping with anxiety. He crept toward the nursery and was about to knock on the door when he heard voices in the hall below. He peered over the banister and saw Laura talking to a huge policeman. The policeman had a truncheon attached to his belt with a large silver whistle peeping out of his top pocket. He was writing down what Laura told him in a notebook.

"Well, miss," he said at last, "we've made full inquiries about Mr. 'Amilton, but we 'aven't managed to trace 'is movements after 'e left the meetin' at four thirty P.M. yesterday. But don't you worry, miss. If any 'arm 'ad come to 'im, we should 'ave 'eard of it by now. 'E'll be safe an' sound, you may be sure. But we'll continue makin' inquiries all the same."

As soon as the policeman had left, Laura quickly seized her cloak and bonnet from a little anteroom and slipped into the street. Raymond followed her at once, but the streets were so crowded that for a long time he was unable to catch up with her. He just about managed to keep in sight of her green bonnet as it bobbed its way in front of him. Where could she be going? he wondered. And where could Mr. Hamilton possibly be? Laura had said he was the kindest father in the world, so he couldn't

have been so cruel as to leave her alone all night without even
sending a message. Therefore he must be in some kind of
danger. But *what* kind?

Raymond was so preoccupied with these thoughts that for a
while he hardly noticed the passersby. Then he began to realize
that most of the people in the street were pale thin men in
ragged clothes, hanging around as if they had nothing to do and
nowhere to go. There were women too, wearing clogs and
threadbare gowns, some of them carrying babies wrapped in the
folds of their shawls. Turning a corner, Raymond heard a sound
of music and came across a whole family—father, mother, and
four children—standing together on the edge of the pavement
and singing, while the smallest child held out a tattered cap to
collect coins from passersby. The tune was very sad but beautiful, like Wally's trumpet, and in spite of his hurry and anxiety
Raymond paused a moment to listen to the words:

> "There is a green hill far away
> Without a city wall
> Where our dear Lord was crucified—
> He died to save us all.
>
> "He died that we might be forgiven,
> He died to make us good,
> That we might go at last to heaven
> Saved by his precious blood."

As he ran on, Raymond thought about that "green hill far
away." It reminded him of the moors surrounding Blackstone,
where sometimes, before he became ill, his mother had taken
him for picnics on sunny days. He could see those moors now,
rising above and beyond the mills and chimneys of the town, and
it struck him as strange that though the town itself had changed
a lot in the hundred years between Laura's time and his own,
the hills all around looked just the same. But he had no time to
continue with these thoughts because Laura suddenly turned

down a narrow side street, and he had to double his speed to keep her in sight.

The street was long and gloomy. The tiny cramped houses on each side seemed to have been squashed together so as to fit as many as possible in each row. There were refuse bins on the pavements outside each house, and washing lines were strung across the street, because none of the houses had backyards or even back doors—instead, other rows of tiny houses were built up against their back walls, forming other streets which stretched away on every side, all exactly alike. At the far end of the street in which Laura was running, there were the huge gates of a mill, and the mill itself towered up behind them, a vast sprawling building of blackened stone, with hundreds of blank-looking windows and an immense chimney, making the workers' houses round about look like pixies' huts outside a giant's castle. The name of the mill was painted in large white letters high up on the brickwork of the chimney: "The Grimsdale."

Raymond caught up with Laura just as she turned into the mill gates. Her pretty face was pale with worry, but it lighted up with a smile when she recognized Raymond. Then once again it became serious as she began to explain why she had come to the mill.

"You see, Raymond," she said as they hurried across the wide cobbled mill yard, which was strangely silent and deserted, "Papa came here to a meeting yesterday, and the police have been told that he left at four thirty, *but I don't believe it.* The people he was meeting—Mr. Grimskull, Mr. Grooch, and Mr. Spurge—are his enemies, and I think they lured him here in order to do him some harm."

"Why are they his enemies?" asked Raymond.

"Oh, for lots of reasons. One is that Father is always trying to make things better for the poor people in the mills. They have to work such terribly long hours, you know—ten hours a day, that's sixty hours a week, in most mills—and that means women and quite young boys and girls, not just grown men.

Father wants the government to pass a law saying that people mustn't be made to work so long.

"Another reason why they hate him is that he wants the poor black slaves to be given their freedom in America. That's why he supports Mr. Lincoln and the Northern states. But most of the mill owners want the South to win, because that's where the cotton comes from for the mills, and at the moment Mr. Lincoln's navy is blockading the cotton ports."

By this time they had crossed the big yard and turned into a side door which led into one of the huge factory rooms. The room was low and dark and so cluttered with looms that the children had difficulty in picking their way from one end to the other. In the narrow aisles between the machines, there were piles of wicker "skips," or baskets. Most of them were empty, since no cotton had come into the mill for many months; others were filled with wooden bobbins or rollers of stiff cardboard. Furry layers and webs of dirty cotton waste lay thick on all the looms and in every crack and crevice, giving the place a spooky appearance, as if a ghostly white spider had been silently weaving and were now waiting somewhere in the shadows to pounce on its victims. The two children shuddered and held each other's hand more tightly. Their footsteps made an eerie muffled echo on the wooden floors thick with white dust. A strange, sour, deathly smell—a mixture of oil and dirt and stale cotton waste—hung in the air.

Slowly Raymond and Laura worked their way through each of the vast rooms and sections of the mill one by one: the spinning rooms, weaving rooms, carding rooms, doubling rooms, and many others whose purpose Raymond couldn't recognize. They crept up stone-flagged staircases, in and out of little offices, peering in every place they went for some sign or clue that might lead them to Laura's Father. Finally, exhausted by their search, they sat down forlornly on an upturned skip.

At that moment they heard footsteps at the far end of the room—strange scuffling footsteps, as if something not quite human were coming toward them.

Raymond and Laura crouched down behind the skip in terror. The scuffling noise got louder and louder, and as the Thing approached, they could hear it panting hoarsely. Raymond seized a large wooden bobbin and made ready to attack the monster if it leaped upon them. Then suddenly, around the edge of the skip, appeared not a griffin, nor a pterodactyl, nor a gorilla, nor a minotaur—but the friendly face of Mullinger, his tongue hanging out, his eyes filled with eager excitement. Behind him, being dragged along on the leash, was a hot and perspiring Wally.

"Well, I'll be blowed," said Wally, "what on earth are you two doin' 'ere?"

"We came to look for Papa," said Laura, and then added, in a very little voice that had tears in it, "but he's not here."

"I suspect you're wrong about that, my dear," said Wally. "Mullinger knows more about these matters than we do. I took the liberty of lettin' 'im 'ave a sniff at your father's smokin' jacket, which Mr. Smarmlin' was removin' from the study. As soon as Mullinger picked up the scent, 'e led me—or p'raps I should say yanked me—straight 'ere. And 'e's still 'ot on the trail, as you can see?"

Mullinger's nose was down, and he began tugging Wally along again. The children followed excitedly through several rooms, up a worn staircase, through a stone archway, and into a part of the mill that was obviously much older than the main building. When he reached this part, he became wildly agitated and raced on at such a pace that poor Wally, whose legs were much too short to keep up, had to let go of the leash. Mullinger rushed on to the end of a room full of very old machines, and then, to their amazement, he began snuffling and sniffing and pawing and prancing at a blank stretch of wall.

"Well, Mullinger old friend," said Wally, "you ain't tryin' to tell us, are you, that Mr. 'Amilton went through that there wall—because that's physically impossible."

"It isn't," said Raymond suddenly. "Look!"

In some of the older mills a revolving shaft driven by the main steam engine ran through from room to room, and the various rooms which this single shaft powered were let off for rent to men who owned their own machines but needed power to drive them. These rooms often housed industries other than cotton—such as joinery or tool making—and so they were sealed off from the others, but a wooden panel was often set into the wall where the connecting door had once been.

It was a panel like this that Raymond had spotted, and Mullinger too was now sniffing at it excitedly. There were signs that it had recently been pulled out, but it had been firmly hammered back into place, and try as they might, the children and Wally could not loosen it again. Laura began banging desperately on the panel and after a moment's silence an answering tap came back.

"Papa," she cried, "are you in there, Papa?"

A muffled reply came from the other side. She recognized his voice but could not make out his words. She was dancing up and down in an agony of impatience.

"Oh, we must get to him," she said, "we must, we must!"

A strange gleam came into Wally's eye. "As a professional escape artist, miss, I 'ave a suggestion to make."

"Oh, what is it? Can you help him to get out, can you, can you?"

"No, miss, but *you* can 'elp *me* to get in—then I can 'ave a word with Mr. 'Amilton, and we can make plans accordingly."

"But how can you possibly get in?" cried Raymond. "It's all sealed off."

"Would you oblige me by bendin' down?" said Wally unexpectedly. "Like that—facin' the wall, legs apart, knees half-bent, hands braced on knees. Thank you. Now, miss, up you go on Raymond's back, kneelin' this time and holdin' tight to his shoulders. Mullinger, you know what to do."

Mullinger did know. Before Wally had finished talking, he had scrambled up the human pyramid formed by the two children and positioned himself on top of Laura, with his leash still dangling down. Using the leash as a rope, Wally hauled himself up until he stood on top of Mullinger, from which position he could just reach the machine shaft at the point where it went through the wall. The hole it went through was wider than the shaft itself, but it certainly didn't look big enough to let a human being through, even if that human being happened to be a midget. Wally, however, thought otherwise. Clinging to the shaft like a monkey, he wormed and turned and twisted and squirmed until gradually, inch by inch and wriggle by wriggle, he fed his whole body through the narrow gap as if it had been a piece of rubber tubing. Only his head remained, sticking out of the wall like a gargoyle on an old church. Then that too slowly disappeared.

The children waited and watched. They could hear voices at the other side, but only faintly. After what seemed like hours of waiting, Wally's feet came into view, then legs, body, head. They formed the pyramid again, and he scrambled down.

"How is he?" cried Laura. "Is he all right? Why is he in there? Is there no way out at the other end? Does he want us to call a police officer?"

"No 'arm 'as come to 'im, miss, apart from a little discomfort. 'E was set upon yesterday after the meetin' by a couple of desperate-lookin' characters wearin' masks. They dragged 'im in there an' boarded up all the exits, but it's 'is opinion that Grimskull's behind it all. You see, miss, Grimskull, Grooch, an' Spurge 'ave been secretly in touch with some of the Confederate agents an' 'ave promised to supply them with a warship to make war on Northern ships. The ship is called the *Alabama* and is due to sneak out of the port of Liverpool next Thursday, though our government 'as expressly forbid it. Your papa, 'e knows all about these plans an' was takin' steps to stop 'em—an' that's why they've locked 'im up—they want to keep 'im prisoner till after the *Alabama*'s got clear away."

Laura drank in every word of Wally's report, nodding at the mention of the three mill owners.

"Just as I thought," she said. "We must call the police at once. Come on, we haven't a moment to lose!"

Away they all ran, Mullinger leading, Laura and Raymond following, and Wally bringing up the rear. They tore out of the mill yard and along the crowded streets, until at last they saw in the distance the familiar blue-black helmet of a bobby. He was firmly but kindly persuading the little groups of idle ragged men to move on along the street, when Laura almost flung herself upon him.

"'Ello, 'ello, 'ello," he said. "Wot's all this 'ere, missy, wot's all this 'ere?"

"My papa's locked up in Grimsdale Mill, and we can't get him out, and Mr. Grimskull and Mr. Grooch and Mr. Spurge have done it, and the *Alabama*'s sailing on Thursday, and we've just *got* to get Papa out so that he can stop it and please, please, will you help us?"

The policeman, who had a rubicund face, ginger side-whiskers, and bulging fishlike eyes, opened his mouth to say something and then shut it again. He was a very young policeman and had never before been confronted with an emergency, especially in the shape of a quivering, tearful little girl pouring out a story that made absolutely no sense. He had been taught that he should do one of three things in an emergency: blow his whistle, flourish his truncheon, or take out his notebook. He decided to take out his notebook. By this time, to add to his confusion, he had become aware that the little girl was not alone. She was accompanied by a small boy, a gigantic dog, and a midget. To make matters even more puzzling, the dog was standing on its hind legs.

"Now, missy, first of all I think I'd better take down your name and address, and I think I ought to warn you," he added, suddenly remembering something else he had been taught, "that anything you say will be taken down and may be used in evidence."

"Oh, please don't be so stupid!" pleaded Laura, stamping her foot in her impatience. "There's no time to write things down *now*. Come with us to the mill, and we'll *show* you what we mean!"

But the policeman would not be persuaded. Very slowly and laboriously, sticking out his tongue a little to help him concentrate, he wrote down their names and addresses with the butt of a blunt pencil. Then he added some further notes, which took at least ten minutes, closed his notebook, buttoned it into his tunic pocket, and said:

"Now you all come along to the police station with me and we'll report this matter to the sergeant."

When they arrived at the police station, the sergeant had just sent out to the cook shop for a dozen oysters and a bottle of brown stout. Not until he had demolished this meal did he emerge from his office, fastening up his uniform over his striped flannel shirt (the two middle buttons wouldn't fasten), and adjusting his helmet carefully to look as if he meant business.

"Now, Constable Crumble," he said at last, "let me 'ear your report."

While Police Constable Crumble read out his report in a monotonous singsong voice, the friends were forced to sit and listen in silence, although they were almost bursting with impatience to get back to the mill. Once or twice they tried to interrupt, but it only made matters worse, so in the end they just sat there glumly waiting for the sergeant and the constable to come to a decision.

While they waited, Raymond's eyes wandered vaguely around the walls, which were plastered with notices. Suddenly the words "Wanted for Murder" caught his eye, and, underneath, the picture of a bearded man in the uniform of an American sailor. The whole notice read as follows:

WANTED FOR MURDER
The Government of the United States is offering a
REWARD OF FIFTEEN HUNDRED DOLLARS
for information leading to the arrest of
HIRAM P. HARPER (alias HARPOON HARRY)

who is wanted for the MURDER in Liverpool of United States Agent Henry J. Roebuck, and also for the crime of desertion from the United States Navy, and also for the crime of HIGH TREASON against the United States Government in that he has entered into conspiracy with representatives of the Rebel States to supply them with Armed Warships to wage war against the Loyal States of the Union.

Raymond was about to nudge Laura and draw her attention to this notice when he heard the sergeant saying:

"In view of the evidence we 'ave 'eard, I propose to take immediate action. We shall proceed to investigate Grimsdale Mill with the aid of the fire brigade."

Ten minutes later, Laura and Raymond, feeling rather proud and excited in spite of their anxiety, were riding through the cobbled streets on top of a gleaming red fire engine drawn by two handsome black horses. They clattered into the mill yard and stopped just beside the old wing of the mill where Mr. Hamilton was imprisoned. Under the sergeant's direction, two firemen were to make an entry by ladders through an upper loading bay, while the constable and the children were to go through the building and try to batter the partition panel down with a fireman's ax.

At last, after what seemed to the children an almost endless journey through the rooms full of dead machinery shrouded in dust and cotton fiber, they arrived at the paneled wall. With three strokes of Constable Crumble's ax and a couple of heaves of his brawny shoulder, the panel caved in. Laura and Raymond rushed into the room beyond.

It was empty. During the long delay at the police station, Mr. Hamilton had been taken elsewhere!

3

A PLOT AND A PICNIC

*in which a pleasant picnic is sandwiched between a
pernicious plot perpetrated by a malicious butler and
a brutal murderer.*

Often, as he lay in the basement, Raymond had caught glimpses
of surveyors and engineers taking measurements in the street.
He knew that they were planning to build a new section of
motorway that would run right through from Blackstone to
Liverpool, and that all the houses in his street were due to be
demolished in order to make way for it.

But today was the first time that there had been any signs
that the work was actually about to start. Early in the morning,
before Mrs. Price set off for work, a police van came along, and a
couple of policemen sealed off the street from traffic by putting
"Detour" notices at each end. Then the demolition men moved in
with their bulldozers, cranes, and trucks. Soon Raymond could
hear the crash and thud of falling stone as they attacked the
first house at the other end of the street.

He felt quite excited and pleased by these developments.
Though he had always hated the *thought* of the street's being
demolished, now that it was actually happening he found it was
interesting and even quite enjoyable.

"How far is Liverpool from here?" he asked his mother.

"Oh, thirty or forty miles."

"How long will it take to get there on the new motor-way?"

"Half an hour or so. In the old days it would take a full day if
you went by canal.

"Do you like motorways better than canals?"

36

"Yes and no. Canals were safer and more peaceful. But motorways are quicker and more comfortable. There's a good and a bad side to everything, I guess."

"But are things better now than they were in the old days? Are *people* better, I mean?"

"People? Well, they're better off, I suppose—better houses, better clothes, better jobs—at least in this part of the world. But better *people*—well, I don't know about that, I'm sure."

"I think," said Raymond, "that they were just the same as us really, and we're just the same as them. Except," he added as an afterthought, "for the policemen."

"And what's so different about the policemen?" Mrs. Price laughed.

"They were much more stupid in those days," said Raymond. "That Constable Crumble, for instance. If he hadn't wasted so much time taking down particulars, we might have rescued Laura's father. . . . "

But Mrs. Price wasn't really listening. She was looking at him anxiously and stroking his forehead, which was certainly very hot and feverish. As she did so, she brushed several bits of white fluff from his hair.

"Dear, oh, dear," she said, "you have cotton bits all over you. Anybody'd think you'd been down to the mill."

Raymond didn't reply. He just smiled to himself. Then his mother renewed his jug of lemonade and laid out his tablets on the bedside table.

"You'll be all right until Mrs. Nuttall comes," she said as she put on her rather shabby-looking gray coat and looked around for her old shopping basket. "I've a few errands to do tonight on the way home, and also I've got to call in and pay the rent—but I shan't be very late."

"Don't worry, Mummy," said Raymond, noticing again her tense and anxious expression as she turned to look back at him from the doorway. "I'll be quite all right, you know."

The door closed, and Raymond was left alone. He felt sorry for his mother, always worrying about him and always busy with work and shopping. He wished he could find some way of making her believe that, now that he had met Wally and Mullinger and Laura, he didn't really mind so much about being so ill.

Outside the house a huge truck thundered past, taking the first load of rubble away from the doomed street. The whole basement shuddered with vibrations, and the kitchen screen began to totter.

"Well, I'll be darned," said Wally, appearing at that moment with Mullinger at the basement door. "Talk about the walls of Jericho! It certainly won't take much to blow *these* walls down."

So saying, he raised his trumpet to his lips and blew a long note, gentle but at the same time thrilling and triumphant, which gradually grew into a tune that Raymond knew well.

> And did those feet in ancient time
> Walk upon England's mountains green?
> And was the holy Lamb of God
> On England's pleasant pastures seen?
>
> And did the Countenance Divine
> Shine forth upon these vales and hills?
> And was Jerusalem builded here
> Among these dark Satanic mills?

Before the last note had died away, the screen had disappeared, and Mrs. Porson came bustling forward to greet them.

But it was a different Mrs. Porson. A gayer, more glamorous Mrs. Porson. A fancier, more fashionable Mrs. Porson. A prettier, more palatable Mrs. Porson. A comelier, more cuddlesome Mrs. Porson.

Instead of the huge mobcap she had formerly worn, she now had on a dainty little circlet of lace, revealing a mass of mouse-colored hair newly curled into delicate ringlets. Gone too were the drab gown and shapeless apron. In their place was a well-cut

gingham dress with a pattern of pink roses, surmounted by a
frilly pinafore which looked, on Mrs. Porson's ample front, not
much bigger than a pocket handkerchief. Peeping out from the
bosom of the dress, which was cut fashionably low, was a little
posy holder containing four flowers—a sweet pea, a peony, a
primula, and a daisy.

When Wally saw them, he turned pale and glanced around
furtively for a way of escape. But Mrs. Porson, dropping him a
little curtsy and fluttering her eyelashes, conducted him to a
chair by the kitchen fire and poured him out a pint of porter
that she had placed in readiness.

Wally took a long draft of porter to give him some courage.
Then he said gallantly:

"Allow me to say, ma'am, that you're lookin' mighty 'andsome
today."

Mrs. Porson blushed. This time it was recognizable as a blush
because it started at her bosom, spread up her chest and neck,
merged into her glowing cheeks, which even a liberal sprinkling
of powder had not managed to tone down, and passed up to her
ears, which continued to burn like beacons during the rest of the
conversation.

"Oh, Mr. Wally," she said, giving him a playful tap which
knocked him back in his seat and caused him to swallow nearly
half a pint of porter at one gulp, "it's such a pleasure to 'ave you
'ere again—you and Master Raymond and your dear little dog."

At this, Mullinger, who was reaching up to investigate a large
joint of beef on the top shelf of the cupboard, hastily shrank
down to poodle size and did a couple of nonchalant Frenchified
steps to indicate that he was just strolling around admiring the
scenery.

"And I must say, ma'am," replied Wally, growing more reckless as he downed the porter, "it's a pleasure for me to be in the
company of such a good-lookin' female. Your very good 'ealth,
ma'am!"

Wally drained his glass, and Mrs. Porson refilled it.

"And 'ow is Miss Laura today?" he went on. "I trust she's 'ad some sleep and taken a bite o' food in spite of 'er anxieties."

"Poor little lady, she's no one to turn to in 'er trouble," said
Mrs. Porson. "We've no 'ousekeeper at the moment—the last
one left because she couldn't abide the butler—an' Miss Peach,
the governess, 'as turned religious an' spends most of 'er time
attending' the Dorcas meetin's or 'elpin the minister or prayin' wi'
t' Sisterhood down at t' chapel. So that leaves Mr. Smarmlin' in
charge—an' 'e won't even let Miss Laura come out of 'er room.
Sez she's got to stay there, 'e does, until Mr. 'Amilton's sister
from Dorset comes up to take charge o' things."

"Why won't Mr. Smarmling let Laura come out?" asked
Raymond in surprise.

"I dunno, Master Raymond, but 'e won't. An' wot's more, 'e
won't let anybody go in to 'er either. 'E's got the footman on duty
outside 'er door. 'E sez it's to protect 'er, but I'm sure the poor
little thing needs to be able to talk to somebody. Now you, Mr.
Wally," she said, turning to him with a fond look and fingering
her posy, "if *you* was in charge of this 'ouse, I'm sure everything
would soon be sorted out."

Mrs. Porson clasped Wally's gnarled and knobbly hand in her
own plump and dimpled one and continued to gaze at him
amorously. He was wondering how to escape from both her clasp
and her gaze when a buzzer rang and a small flap clicked down
over the "Butler's Pantry" sign on the brand-new electric
bellboard.

"Drat it!" said Mrs. Porson. "That's Mr. Smarmlin' now. Ever
since this 'lectric gadget were fitted in 'e's bin pressin' 'is bell an'
lordin' it over the rest of us. What can 'e want now? Bit o' chicken
breast, most likely, or a taste o' the fresh cheese-an'-onion pie."

She applied her ear to the speaking tube fixed on the wall. The
butler's rather greasy voice could be heard at the other end of it.
She answered, "Yes, Mr. Smarmlin', no, Mr. Smarmlin', yes,
Mr. Smarmlin'," and then replaced the cap on the tube.

" 'E wants me to send a meal up to Miss Laura in t'nursery. 'E
sez she wouldn't touch a thing 'e offered 'er at dinner last night
or breakfast this morn' but 'e thinks if I send somethin'

tasty up through the nursery servin' 'atch she'll probably eat it. If you ask me, 'e's gettin worried that she might starve 'erself to death while 'e keeps 'er locked up there."

Mrs. Porson bustled about preparing a dainty tray of food—a freshly boiled speckled egg, a plate of crisp buttered toast (which Raymond made by the fire on the long brass-handled toasting fork), a bowl of pineapple jelly covered with fresh cream, and a dishful of gingerbread animals. She popped a little knitted cozy on top of the egg to keep it warm on its journey up through the hatch, and covered the whole tray with a pretty pink napkin on which were embroidered the words:

> Dear Lord, whate'er we drink or eat,
> Help us to be clean and neat.

Finally she put the meal in the nursery hatch and was just about to haul it up when Wally said:

"Excuse me, ma'am, but I'd be much obliged if you'd allow me to go up the 'atch with that tray. Then I can 'ave a word in private with Miss Laura an' perhaps persuade 'er to 'ave a bit to eat. After that you can 'aul me down with the empties, an' Smarmlin'll be none the wiser."

Mrs. Porson hesitated, but her hesitation disappeared when Wally seized her hand with a romantic gesture and pressed it to his lips. A moment later, with rather more puffing and wheezing from Mrs. Porson than usual, the nursery tray and Wally rumbled their way up through the hollow wall of the house.

Ten minutes passed, then fifteen, then twenty. Raymond began to think that Wally would never return. At last he could stand it no longer. Leaving Mullinger asleep before the fire (with his back legs stretched out in a most unpoodlelike position) and Mrs. Porson busy with the midday meal, he slipped away up the stairs that led to the main part of the house.

He had just emerged into the wide hall and was about to dart up to the first landing when he saw two chambermaids coming down the stairs. Quickly he slipped into a room that led off the hall, and waited until the coast was clear.

It was a large room, lined with glass-fronted bookcases, with a handsome oak desk in front of the window and a comfortable leather sofa facing the fireplace. This must be Mr. Hamilton's study. Raymond gazed around it, his curiosity getting the better of him. He had never seen so many things in one room before— so many books, so many pictures, so many newspapers, so many pens, penholders, letters, letter racks, paperweights, pipes, pipe cases, tobacco jars, snuffboxes, smokers' cabinets, filing cabinets, bureaus, busts, bulletins—in short, so many of all the assorted odds and ends of furniture and ornaments and bits and pieces that Raymond's mother said "make the house look a pickle and need more dusting than they're worth." The strange thing was, though, that Mr. Hamilton's study *didn't* look a pickle. Everything seemed to be tidy and organized—yet not *too* tidy either. It was a studious, serious, hardworking room—but also a cozy and a jolly one. How nice it must be, Raymond thought, to have a father, especially one so kind and sensible as Mr. Hamilton.

He was just about to venture out of this fascinating room when he heard voices again in the hall outside. Then, to his horror, the door began to open. He looked around in a panic for somewhere to hide. There was only one place—behind the thick velvet curtains which reached from ceiling to floor in the wide bay window. He had just time to dodge behind them when the door opened wide, and two people entered.

One of them, whose voice Raymond immediately recognized as Mr. Smarmling's, was saying:

"Have no fear, sir, we shall be quite private in here. Mr. Hamilton is hardly likely to interrupt us"—he said this with a fat, unpleasant chuckle—"and I've taken steps to ensure that that busybody little daughter of his is not likely to interfere with our plans again either. In fact, you may make yourself quite at home, sir. Have a cigar. May I recommend one of Mr. Hamilton's excellent Havanas? And perhaps you'll join me in a glass of his rather choice port?"

Raymond heard the clink of glasses and the glug-glug of wine being poured from a decanter. Then there was a fizzy crackle which sounded like the striking of one of the large club-headed cigar matches, which he had noticed in a little jar on the walnut bureau. The two men smoked and drank for a moment in silence. Then Mr. Smarmling began to speak again:

"Yes, indeed, sir, everything is going according to plan. Mr. Grimskull has been in touch with Capitan Semmes, who is to take command of the *Alabama,* and Mr. Grooch has contacted his agents in Liverpool, who are confident that they can find some gunners for her. She's well stocked for the voyage, and everything will be ready for her to slip away on Thursday. All this has been done under the very nose of the customs officers and the Yankee detectives, yet nobody suspects a thing— nobody, that is, except Mr. Hamilton, and he doesn't count anymore."

Then the other man spoke for the first time. His voice was rather deep, and he had the nasal drawl of an American: "Lucky you found out about Hamilton. He could have ruined everything. How did you know that he was getting suspicious?"

Mr. Smarmling gave another fat chuckle. "Quite simple, my dear sir, quite simple. It happens to be one of my duties to bring in Mr. Hamilton's mail each morning, and when I saw a number of letters bearing New York and Liverpool postmarks, my suspicions were aroused. Then one day I happened to be going through the pockets of Mr. Hamilton's smoking jacket—with a view to having the garment *cleaned,* you understand, sir"— again came the fat chuckle—"when to my great surprise I discovered one of the letters in question. That letter was from the American agent Roebuck—whom I believe you too had, how shall I put it?—some, er, *dealings* with, sir—and I lost no time in communicating the contents of it to Mr. Grimskull."

There was another pause while the glasses were refilled. Then the butler continued:

"All that remains now is for the final detailed arrangements to be made for the sailing of the *Alabama.* These arrangements are being made today between Captain Semmes and Mr.

Spurge, and they will be communicated to you if you will present yourself at Mr. Grimskull's residence—Grimskull Lodge, Moorland Road—between ten and ten thirty this evening. These directions will guide you there by way of the back streets, since I presume you do not wish to be too—er—conspicuous at the moment."

There was a rustle of paper as Mr. Smarmling handed his visitor a map of the district. Then he went on:

"And now, sir, just before you leave, perhaps you will join me in a toast. To the success of the *Alabama* and the Southern Confederacy!"

At this moment Raymond ventured to peep through a chink in the curtains. The person whom he saw raising his glass to Mr. Smarmling's toast was, though now clean-shaven and dressed in civilian clothes, none other than Hiram P. Harper, alias Harpoon Harry!

Raymond waited until Mr. Smarmling and Harpoon Harry had left the room and their voices had died away along the passage. Then he crept out of his hiding place and poked his head out of the door to see if it was safe to emerge. He had just decided that it was, and had started to tiptoe along the hall, when he heard the thud of flying feet on the landing above. A moment later the footman came hurtling down the stairs, crashed into an umbrella stand in the hall, and shot out of the front door like a bullet from a gun. Close on his heels was a flying mass of ferocious brown-and-black fur, which followed the footman out into the street and then reappeared at the door in the more familiar shape of Mullinger. At the same moment Wally and Laura came quickly down the stairs. Without even pausing to pick up the shattered umbrella stand, the four friends made their escape through the front door.

They ran swiftly along the street for fear of pursuit and didn't slow down until they came to the center of the town, where they could mingle with the crowds. The stalls were set out on the cobbled market square, but there were more people gazing longingly at the goods than actually buying them. Wally bought a meat pie and gave it to a group of ragged, half-starved children. He also bought a blood sausage for Mullinger.

"You've earned that, old friend," he said as Mullinger gulped down the succulent globules of pig meat. "Nothing but the rage of the Mighty Mullinger could 'ave shifted that there footman."

The Mighty Mullinger licked his lips, wagged his tail, and smiled.

By this time Raymond had recovered his breath sufficiently to tell his friends what he had overheard in Mr. Hamilton's study. Wally nodded as if he had guessed it all along. A look of deep concern came over Laura's face.

"But . . . if that horrible man is a . . . a murderer, do you think he might be going to . . . ?"

A sob prevented her from finishing her sentence. Raymond put his arm around her, but the kind look in his eyes made her sob even more.

"There, there, miss," said Wally. "You mustn't be thinkin' thoughts like that. If old Grimskull had intended any actual bodily 'arm to your papa, 'e'd 'ave done it before now. No, you can take it from me that all 'e wants to do is to keep Mr. 'Amilton out o' the way until the *Alabama* 'as sailed. Then 'e'll 'ave 'im set free an' pretend 'e 'ad nothing to do with it. Now, instead of 'angin' around and worryin' about things that ain't goin' to 'appen, we can draw up a plan of campaign. *Where* is this 'Arpoon 'Arry goin' to get 'is instructions, Raymond?"

"Grimskull Lodge."

"Ah, I know the place. It's right up on the edge of the moors. Now why don't we three and Mullinger 'ere make our way up to the moors and spend the day picnickin' in the sunshine? Nobody's likely to come lookin' for us up there, that's certain! Then at nightfall we'll creep down and see what we can see at that old Grimskull Lodge."

At the word "picnic" Raymond's eyes began to sparkle, and even Laura's pale tear-stained face brightened up. She took out a little silk purse from the pocket of her pinafore dress and began to count her money. It came to one shilling and sixpence three farthings. Next, from another pocket, she produced a small notebook and a tiny pencil. The notebook was entitled "A Little Girl's Book of Thrift," and at the top of each of the pages, which were ruled out in pounds, shillings, and pence columns, was a little motto like:

"Waste not, want not" or "A penny saved is a penny gained."

On a new page of the notebook Laura now made a list of those items she intended to buy for the picnic, and as Wally and Raymond came back with each of these items in turn, she entered the price in the money column. At last the page read like this:

1 large pork pie	5d
1 large bottle dandelion and burdock	2d
1 jar potted meat	1½d
6 fresh muffins	3d
¼ lb. Lancashire cheese	2d
6 cream puffs	3d
3 oat cakes	¾d
4 toffee apples	1d
½ oz. peppermint drops	¼d
TOTAL	1s 6½d

There was just one farthing left, and this Laura gave to Raymond, entering it duly in her notebook:

Gift to Raymond for services rendered	¼d

Feeling content with their purchases and eager to begin the feast, they set out at a brisk pace on the long road that went winding out of the town to the moors.

The picnic was a great success. They chose a sunny spot in the corner of a field, sheltered by the dry stone wall from the cool breeze that creeps over these moors even on the sunniest days. All around them as far as the eye could see stretched the great humps of granite and millstone grit formed by upheavals of the earth's crust hundreds of centuries before either Raymond or Laura, or Queen Victoria or Mr. Lincoln, or motorways or cotton mills, or England or America were ever heard of. These massive rocks were covered with rough grass, bracken, and heather, with here and there a clump of trees twisted into strange shapes by the strong whistling wind. Raymond felt happy lying on his back in the snug shelter of the wall, licking a toffee apple or munching an oat cake and gazing up at the high sky with its slow-moving procession of white clouds. Somewhere almost as high as those clouds, a skylark was pouring out its tiny sweet-sounding song, and from time to time across the open hills the snickering voices of sheep could be heard as they nibbled their way up to the higher ridges.

It was a long, lazy day in which time seemed to stand still, and they forgot their troubles in the joy of being together in the warm bright air. Tired out with the strain of the previous two days, Laura fell asleep snuggled up against Mullinger, with her head resting upon his soft furry flank. Then when she woke up, they all had a race to the top of a high tor where there was a squat stone lookout tower built way back in the time of the Napoleonic wars. As they ran over the springy moorland turf, Laura shouted, "Last to the top pays a forfeit!" Mullinger easily won the race and stood at the top barking gleefully while Laura panted up after him, followed by Raymond, with Wally as usual trotting along in the rear. When they had all got their breath back, Laura and Raymond announced Wally's forfeit, which was, of course, to play a tune on his trumpet. Wally scrambled up onto the parapet of the lookout tower and gazed for a moment across the moors to the west, where, in the far distance, a thin bright ribbon of light showed where Lancashire met the sea. Then he winked at the children, put his trumpet to his lips, and played a tune which Raymond remembered his mother having sung to him sometimes when he was very small:

Blow the wind southerly, southerly, southerly,
Blow the wind south o'er the bonny blue sea.
Blow the wind southerly, southerly, southerly,
Blow, bonny breezes, my lover to me.

They told me last night there were ships in the offing
And I hurried down to the deep rolling sea,
But my eye did not see it wherever might be it—
The bark that is bearing my true love to me.

When the last clear notes of the trumpet had died away, they
were all silent for a few moments, each one thinking his own
thoughts. Then Wally broke the silence:

"Now then, all of you, best foot forward. We've a long way to go
if we want to get to Grimskull Lodge before nightfall."

Wally was right. They had come a lot farther on the moors
than they had realized, and as they picked their way back
toward the town, following the packhorse trails past the old
weavers' cottages with their funny high attics where the looms
used to be kept, the night clouds came up all around them, and
they shuddered a little at the thought of what lay ahead.

At last they got back onto the main road, which dropped
steeply toward the edge of the town. The gas lights twinkled in
the town center, but up here on the side of the moor everything
was shrouded in darkness. Soon, the dark outline of Grimskull
Lodge came into view. It was a lonely house, approached by a
long drive flanked by enormous boulders hewn out of the nearby
quarry. The house itself was built of black stone and looked
more like a fortress than a private house. All the walls had
battlements, and at one corner of the building rose an ugly
square tower. As Wally and the children crept across the shrubbery of dark leathery-leaved rhododendron bushes, they noticed
that the top half of this tower contained a room, with windows
on all four sides, and through the chinks of the curtains of this
room they could see a light—the only light that was visible in
the whole house.

At that moment they heard the sound of footsteps coming up the drive. A man was approaching the house. They shrank back into the bushes and watched as he clattered the brass knocker on the thick iron-studded front door. After several moments, the door opened, and Mr. Grimskull himself appeared. In the light of the lamp which he held in his hand, the children could make out his harsh bony face and deep-set eyes, surmounted by a bald head as rough and craggy as the boulders in his drive. A few tufts of wiry iron-gray hair still sprouted behind his ears, like the stunted furze or hawthorn bushes up on the bare moors. And the same light that revealed Grimskull to them also revealed the face of his visitor, a face by now all too familiar to Raymond— the brutal face of Harpoon Harry. Then the door closed, and all was darkness once more.

At once Wally darted forward to the side of the tower. Half-way up, just below the level of the upper windows, there was a projecting stone slab on which were carved the words "Grimskull Lodge 1811" and below them a Latin motto: *"Pecunia Omnia Vincit"* (wealth conquers all).

There was a straggly growth of ivy just beneath the ledge, and it was this that Wally was looking at intently when the children and Mullinger crept up to him. At once they knew what was in his mind and, without waiting to be told, they formed their three-tier pyramid of boy, girl, and dog. Wally scrambled up, seized the ivy, and in no time at all was crouching on the ledge with his eye and ear close to the chink in the curtains of the lighted room.

The watchers below looked up with bated breath. The ledge was so narrow that Wally had to press himself into the stonework with arms outspread, his fingertips clutching tiny wisps of ivy, which threatened every moment to tear away from the wall. Twice he began to slide off the ledge and only managed to save himself by clutching at the rusty iron staples that had been driven into the cement to support the ivy. Finally, when even these began to work loose, Wally decided that he had seen and heard enough. Quick as a cat, he came slithering and sluthering down the wall, using every crack and crevice as a momentary hold. The last six feet he took in one mighty jump, turning a complete somersault before landing upright in a bed of dock leaves.

"Harper will be coming out in a moment," he whispered. "He'll be carrying a small portfolio in which Grimskull has given him detailed instructions about how and where to join the *Alabama*. We must get hold of that portfolio."

"But how?" cried Laura and Raymond, with one voice.

"Oh, it's quite simple," replied Wally, with such a cheery wink that they could even see it in the blackness of the shrubbery. "It's quite simple—we're going to ambush him as he goes down the drive!"

It might have seemed simple to Wally, but it seemed terrifying to Laura and Raymond. How could two children and a midget ambush a murderer? With sinking hearts they followed Wally as he led them almost jauntily down the drive.

About two hundred yards from the house, the rocky bank on each side of the drive rose so high that the drive itself seemed almost like a railway track going through a deep cutting. The black bitter soil in which these flanking rocks were embedded contained minerals which favored the growth of rhododendrons, and so from the sides and top of the bank, huge bushes grew, reaching out in places to form a dense roof of foliage over the drive below. It was here that Wally stopped.

"Right now, this is the plan. When Harper comes down, I'll drop on him from the bushes above. 'E'll 'ave to let go of the portfolio when 'e feels me legs locked round 'is neck in a viselike grip. Raymond and Laura, that'll be your chance. Grab the portfolio and run! Make for the quarry up on the moor behind the house. Then, when I release me victim, Mullinger'll 'old 'im at bay till I get clear off, won't you, Mullinger, me lad?"

Mullinger agreed enthusiastically, jerking his head and pawing the ground as if to say, "Let's have less talk and more action." He didn't have to wait very long for the action. Almost before the ambushers had had time to position themselves,

Harpoon Harry came swaggering down the drive. He was whistling "Dixie" slightly out of tune, and had just got to the chorus part—"Look away, look away, look away, Dixieland"— when Wally landed neatly on his shoulders.

Crossing his legs around the man's neck and grabbing his ears, which were the large, sticking-out kind, Wally hung on for dear life. With a cry of pain and alarm, Harper dropped the portfolio and tried to shake off his attacker, but Wally twisted his ears so hard that all he could do was dance up and down in agony. With Wally riding Harper like a cowboy on a bucking bronco, Laura and Raymond grabbed the portfolio and made off with it down the drive. Wally gave them several minutes to get clear, then leaped neatly out of his saddle, leaving Mullinger to take over the next phase of the operation.

But now the first snag appeared in Wally's plan. Harper was armed. At first he had been too concerned about rescuing his ears to remember his pistol, but now he drew it forth from the inside pocket of his frock coat and aimed at the retreating Wally. In the nick of time Mullinger leaped up and seized his wrist, and the shot went wide. The pistol clattered to the ground, but Wally knew that Mullinger would be in grave danger if Harper managed to retrieve it, so he gave a sharp whistle, and Mullinger, with a final snap at Harper's groping fingers, came bounding away. Wally had a start but not a big one, so Harper picked up his pistol and set off in pursuit. By the time Wally and Mullinger got to the quarry where the children were anxiously waiting, Harper was only a few seconds behind them.

Once they had entered the quarry, which was cut deep into the side of a large hill, there seemed to be no escape. The black rock rose up sheer on all sides; there was hardly a foothold for a mountain sheep. But as they ran blindly toward the rock face, Wally's boot crunched on something softer than the hard stones that littered the floor of the quarry. Bending down quickly, he picked something up. It was a lump of coal!

"They may be working a coal seam here," he whispered. "Look for a tunnel."

It was Mullinger who found the tunnel, but as they darted

into it, they knew that Harpoon Harry had spotted them. What would he do? Would he follow them down that blind hole in the earth, as a ferret follows a rabbit, and trap them when they could go no farther? Or would he wait at the mouth of the tunnel and shoot them down when they ventured to reappear? As they ran deeper and deeper into the blackness, it seemed certain that one way or another they were doomed. The only consolation was that since the passage was very low and very narrow—only just about big enough, in fact, for *them* to pass through without stooping—Harpoon Harry would be slowed up if he decided to follow them in.

Then even *that* consolation disappeared as they heard a clanking sound near the mouth of the tunnel. Harry was following them in one of the iron trucks that ran on the single-track line beneath their feet. This was worse than being trapped or shot down! They would be crushed to death by the heavy iron car as it came hurtling down the steep incline. Already they could hear it gathering speed. Faster and faster it came on, faster and louder, louder and faster, until the noise rose to a deafening pitch. They huddled together in panic and despair, awaiting the terrible moment of impact. Then suddenly and incredibly, the hideous noise seemed to grow less, and then less again, until gradually it faded away to a distant clank somewhere to their right.

The tunnel must have forked, back there a way. In their mad scramble through the darkness, they hadn't noticed. They had taken the left fork, but Harpoon Harry had gone careering off down the right. By the time he realized his mistake, they would be safely away from the quarry, well out of reach of his murderous pistol.

4
KIDNAPPERS AND A CONSTABLE

in which a churchgoing governess turns out to be not as pious as she appears, and the ponderous policeman flourishes his truncheon to no avail.

"I can't imagine how you get your hands so black—and you in bed all day long!"

It was Sunday morning, and Mrs. Price was taking longer than usual over Raymond's wash and brushup, since she didn't have to hurry off to work. Raymond too was enjoying the lazy feeling he always got on Sunday morning, even though all the days were alike for him. It was nice to see his mother puttering around in her old flowered dressing gown, frizzling herself a bit of bacon and browsing through the thick Sunday newspaper while she ate it.

Raymond liked the newspaper, though these days he usually felt too weary to struggle in bed folding and unfolding its big pages. Still, it was nice to see it lying around the flat, packed with the latest stories and pictures from all over the world. It made him feel that the world outside was going on in the same way as usual—people winning fortunes, exploring space, signing treaties, fighting wars, designing new fashions, getting married, becoming famous, dying. . . . Somehow the newspaper made even the strange and frightening things seem safe and ordinary.

Today, though, there wasn't any really exciting news. It was mostly about things he didn't understand, like the economic crisis or the Common Market. His eye caught sight of a head-line: "Government Freeze to Last till August," and he asked, "Mummy, how can the government make it freeze in summer?"

Mrs. Price laughed. "No, dear. You don't understand. It doesn't mean freeze in that sense. It means that the government is trying to stop the prices of things rising all the time."

"Why are they always rising?"

"I don't know, I'm sure, but they are. Why, when I was a girl, a bar of chocolate was two pence. Now it's five new pence, which is a shilling. Yesterday I paid ten new pence for a quarter pound of Lancashire cheese! Disgusting, I call it!"

"Yes," said Raymond thoughtfully, "a hundred years ago you could have got that cheese for twopence, which was less than one new penny. And you could get an oat cake or half an ounce of peppermints for a farthing!"

"It's funny to hear you talking about farthings," said Mrs. Price. "They were going out of use even in *my* time."

"I've got one," said Raymond. "Laura gave it to me."

"I daresay you have, dear," said Mrs. Price vaguely.

She tidied away the breakfast things and sat down with her knitting by Raymond's bedside. But the strain of working each day and often having to sit up with Raymond far into the night was making her very tired, and soon her knitting slipped from her hands and she dozed off.

Raymond gazed up at the window. Hardly any feet were passing this morning—just an odd pair of slippers shuffling around to the newsstand or, very occasionally, a well-polished pair of shoes striding out to church. But since the church down the street had been demolished and the one around the corner turned into a warehouse, there were fewer churchgoers than ever to be seen these days. There was always the Salvation Army, though—and here they were, marching around the corner and into Raymond's street.

They stopped just outside the area railings and got ready to play. Raymond tried to guess from their legs which ones played which instruments. The short fat legs must belong to the tuba players and the long thin ones to the trombonists. But there were so many legs that it was impossible to sort them all out, and anyway the music was beginning, so it was nicer just to lie back and listen:

> Amazing grace, how sweet the sound
> That save a wretch like me;
> I once was lost but now am found,
> Was blind but now I see.
>
> Through many dangers, trials, and woes
> I have already gone,
> But grace has led me safe through those
> And grace will lead me on.

Raymond began to think of the "many dangers, trials and woes" that he was going through with Laura, but at that moment there was a change in the music and instead of the whole band a single trumpet was playing the last verse of the hymn:

> When we've been there ten thousand years
> Bright-shining as the sun,
> There'll be more ways to sing His praise
> Than when we first begun.

There was no mistaking Wally's trumpet, and the next moment Wally himself, wearing a Salvation Army hat, appeared at the door with Mullinger, who was carrying a collecting bag.

"Anything for the Sally Army, sir?" he grinned, as Mullinger jingled the bag and advanced into the room.

Raymond fumbled under his pillow and produced a very tiny coin. On one side there was the head of a queen and the inscription: *"Dei Gratia Regina Victoria."* On the other side there was a stamp of Britannia ruling the waves, and the words: *"Fid. Def. Ind. Imp.* One Farthing 1862."

"Well," said Wally, examining the coin carefully and biting it to see if it was genuine, "if that's all you can afford, we'd best slip back of this screen, where it's likely to buy a good deal more than it is here."

So saying, he drew aside the screen, revealing the sad spectacle of Mrs. Porson in floods of tears at the kitchen table, being comforted by Laura.

"It's no good, miss," sobbed Mrs. Porson. "'E's gone and 'e won't nivver come back to me. I know 'e won't. I can feel it in me bones." Mrs. Porson felt vaguely around her well-padded anatomy for some sign of a bone, but failing to find any, she put her hand over her heart instead and went on:

"Me 'eart's broken. Things were nivver the same as this with Mr. Porson. 'E were a good man an' 'e looked after me well, but I nivver lost me 'eart to 'im in the way I 'ave to Mr. Wally."

Mrs. Porson burst into fresh sobs as she thought of her lost heart. Laura seized her hand and said:

"Dear Cook, don't think these sad thoughts. Mr. Wally's sure to come again soon—and so is . . . Raymond," she added, her blue eyes softening as she shyly mentioned his name.

Wally glanced around nervously as if looking for a way of retreat, but Raymond ran forward eagerly.

"Of course we've come back," he cried. "We're not going to leave you ever, are we, Wally?"

Wally hesitated and then decided to make the best of a bad job.

"Of course not, ma'am," he said, springing to attention and bringing his hand up to his Salvation Army hat in a smart salute. "We're always at your service, ma'am—and yours, Miss Laura."

Mrs. Porson's red face, made redder by sobbing, became redder still when she realized that Wally had witnessed her outburst. Then her embarrassment turned to admiration and she cried:

"Oh, Mr. Wally, 'ow 'andsome you look in your new 'at!"

"Thank you, ma'am," said Wally. "It's the uniform of a new religious mission to 'elp the poor. Not that I'm turnin' *religious, ma'am,*" he added hastily as a shadow of anxiety crossed Mrs. Porson's face, "but I like to blow me trumpet, and I'd as soon blow it for the poor as for the rich."

"That's all right then," said Mrs. Porson, although she still looked rather doubtful. "I don't 'old with too much religion. All these new churches they're buildin'—there's one goin' up just down the street an' another one round the corner—at this rate there'll soon be more churches than people."

"But churches are . . . nice," said Raymond. "At least they're nicer than—" He was going to say "warehouses and motorways," but he changed his mind and ended lamely, "Anyway, I quite like them."

"They're all right sometimes," said Laura, "like harvest festivals and Christmas. But Miss Peach makes me go three times every Sunday, and in between the services I have to learn collects and texts and the only book I'm allowed to read is the Bible and the only game I'm allowed to play with is my Noah's Ark jigsaw puzzle."

Raymond thought the Noah's Ark jigsaw puzzle sounded rather nice but instead of saying so he asked: "Will you have to go to church today?"

"Yes. That's the only reason why Mr. Smarmling has let me out of my room. He still doesn't suspect where I went yesterday, and he's asked Miss Peach to keep an eye on me today. But she's gone to an early prayer meeting before morning service, so I've slipped down here to see you and ask Wally if he's sorted through the papers in Harper's portfolio yet."

"Yes, miss," said Wally. "The portfolio is safely hidden away, but I've got the papers right here."

He unbuckled his khaki knapsack and laid out a sheaf of documents on the kitchen table. Most of them were maps of various wharves in the Liverpool and Birkenhead shipyards, together with tide tables and sketches of currents and shipping lanes in the River Mersey. Wally pushed these to one side and drew attention to just one letter. It was written in a bold flowing hand and addressed to:

Enoch Grimskull Esq.
Grimskull Lodge
Blackstone

The children began to read:

Dear Sir,

By arrangement with my government, I have agreed to take command of the merchant destroyer *Alabama*. I understand that she is at present berthed in No. 12 Wharf at Laird's Birkenhead shipyard. If you arrange for her to move out into the Mersey River for trials on Thursday 23rd July, taking the first tide, I shall arrange to board her from a tug boat with an American pilot who knows the river well. As soon as we are aboard we shall proceed to sea at full speed before the British dockyard police and the Yankee detectives suspect our intentions. I shall then set course for the Azores, where, I understand, my Government has made arrangements for the ship to be fitted out with full armament.

The enclosed maps and tide tables will assist the First Mate of the Birkenhead crew in moving the *Alabama* out of the yards and into position to proceed to sea next Thursday.

Thank you for your valuable co-operation in this matter. With a powerful vessel like the *Alabama* at our disposal, we are certain to be able to carry the war home to the Yankees.

Yours faithfully,
(Capt.) RAPHAEL SEMMES

P.S. Please instruct Mr. Harper to join the *Alabama* at the Liverpool wharf. If he can bring Charles Hamilton as hostage, so much the better. Such a hostage will ensure both his own safety and that of the ship until we are clear of the Azores.

The children gazed in horror at this letter, especially at the last sentences of the postscript, but before they had time to discuss it the thin reedy voice of Miss Peach was heard calling down the kitchen steps for Laura.

Miss Peach was thin and thirty. Her nose was like a beak, her fingers like claws. Behind her rimless spectacles glittered eyes as hard as stones. She was dressed in a straight gray coat covering a straight gray skirt and stiff white blouse with starched collar. Her hair was completely hidden under a large straw bonnet shaped like a bucket. She came down the kitchen steps carrying Laura's best blue pelisse and ribboned boater. Mullinger growled when he saw her.

"Get these on, child," she said to Laura, "and be quick about it. It is not becoming for a young lady to spend her time gossiping with the servants, especially on Sunday morning. 'Every idle word that men shall speak, they shall give account thereof in the day of judgment.'—Saint Matthew, Chapter Twelve, Verse Thirty-Six."

She dragged Laura roughly into her clothes, thrust a prayer book into her hand, and whisked her away up the steps. Raymond, Wally, and Mullinger dodged out by the basement door and followed them at a safe distance along the street.

At length they turned into the porch of a large church. Raymond, Wally, and Mullinger began to follow them in, but as they crept into the dim and crowded aisle, a portly figure in pinstripe trousers and frock coat loomed up to bar their way. It was Mr. Smarmling, looking more greasy and pompous than ever in his capacity as chief usher.

"No dogs allowed," he growled, glaring at Mullinger, then adding as he caught sight of Wally, "and the same applies to dwarfs."

Wally shrugged his shoulders, winked at Raymond, stuck out his tongue at the enraged Smarmling, and ran off with Mullinger across the churchyard, leapfrogging the tombstones as he went. Raymond hesitated, wondering whether to follow him, but decided instead to stay and wait for Laura. He slipped into a pew behind a thick pillar, unnoticed by Smarmling.

Smarmling in fact was too busy ushering well-dressed ladies and gentlemen to their pews to take any further thought about Raymond. He glided up and down the aisles with a solemn simper on his face, his head cocked slightly to one side and his pale plump hands clasped piously together. He distributed hymn books, posted up the numbers of the psalms, arranged the book markers in the Bible at the big brass lectern, tidied up the papers in the vicar's stall, fussed around in the pulpit, and scolded the assembled choirboys for shuffling their feet. Finally the vicar entered, and the service began.

What a long service it was! There were five psalms, eight hymns, three long Bible readings, an anthem, innumerable prayers, an endless string of church notices and—longer than all the rest put together, or so it seemed to Raymond—a slow, turgid, dull, dragging sermon. At first Raymond thought the sermon was going to be nice, because it began with an interesting story that he had not heard before:

> Now when he came nigh to the gate of the city, behold, there was a dead man carried out, the only son of his mother, and she was a widow: and much people of the city was with her. And when the Lord saw her he had compassion on her, and said unto her, Weep not. And he came and touched the bier: and they that bare him stood still. And he said, Young man, I say unto thee, Arise. And he that was dead sat up, and began to speak. And he delivered him unto his mother.

Raymond liked the funny old-fashioned words of the story and the way Jesus spoke so simply and briefly—just a few short words like "Weep not" and "Arise." He liked the bit too where the dead man sat up, and began to speak. What would he have spoken about? Would he have told them what it had felt like to be dead? Or would he have asked his mother why he was being carried through the streets on a stretcher with "much people of the city" all around him? But these were not the things that interested the preacher. He said the story was not really about a young man at all but about something called "regeneration" and "justification." He used so many big words to explain it that Raymond ended up feeling that the Bible was as hard to understand as the economic crisis or the Common Market.

At long last the service ended, and the people began to move slowly out. Some, however, stayed behind to say extra prayers, and among these was Miss Peach. Raymond waited and waited, but still she knelt on her hassock with stiff back and bowed head, while Laura shuffled impatiently beside her. Finally, when everyone had left, Smarmling came out of the vestry where he had been tidying away the hymn books and said in a voice that echoed strangely through the silent empty church:

"Georgiana, bring the child here!"

Miss Peach seized Laura firmly and began to propel her toward the vestry. From his hiding place behind the pillar, Raymond could see the cruel glint in her eye as well as the expression of doting adoration that came into her face as she approached Smarmling.

"Horace," she murmured, stroking his arm fondly. "Everything is in readiness. I have booked the railway tickets and packed the jewelry and silverware in a trunk and arranged for its collection as you instructed." Then she added as an afterthought, " 'All things are lawful unto me'—First Corinthians, Chapter Six, Verse Twelve."

"You have done well, my dear. We are doing no more than taking what is due to us from a master who has treated us unjustly by impoverishing himself. 'Make to yourselves friends of the mammon of unrighteousness'—Saint Luke, Chapter Sixteen, Verse Nine."

"But how shall we dispose of the child?" asked Miss Peach. "She cannot be allowed her freedom until we are safely abroad."

"My friend Mr. Harper has plans to send her on a little sea voyage, together with her dear father, whose whereabouts she is so keen to discover. In fact, Mr. Harper is due to arrive here any moment," he said, glancing at a large watch which he took from a pocket in his bulging waistcoat.

Sobbing more with anger than with fear, Laura began to kick and struggle to get away. One glorious kick landed with a sharp crack on Miss Peach's bony shin, causing her to release her grip momentarily. Smarmling made a grab for Laura, but at that moment Raymond decided to charge. With his head down, he went straight for Smarmling's waistcoat and hit it fairly in the middle with a soft thud. The butler uttered a gasp and sank down like a punctured balloon. Leaving him to the tender care of Miss Peach, Raymond and Laura raced down the center aisle, through the little porch, and out into the sunlight.

There they ran smack into a man who was just about to enter the church. He grabbed them, one in each of his hairy fists, and, looking up, they found they were gazing into the face of Hiram P. Harper.

An unpleasant grin spread over Harper's face. He twisted the children's arms up behind their backs and began to march them into the church porch. But just as he was about to enter, a blue-uniformed arm descended on his shoulder and a voice said:

"Wot's all this 'ere, then, wot's all this 'ere?"

It was P. C. Crumble, accompanied by Wally and Mullinger, who had spotted Harper lurking in the churchyard and gone in search of help. It had taken them so long to convince the constable that they had seen the wanted murderer, whose picture was hanging in the police station, that in the end they had arrived almost too late. But now at last they were here, and the constable dragged Harper into the sunlight and eyed him narrowly with what he fondly imagined to be a piercing glance. Then he took out his notebook and pencil (which had become even smaller and blunter) and prepared to begin an interrogation.

"Your name an' address, if you please, sir?" he said, his pencil poised and his tongue already protruding slightly.

"John Smith," said Harper quickly. "Sixty-six High Street . . . er . . . London."

The constable entered these details in his book and then once again fixed Harper with his fishlike gaze.

"I should say you'd lived in Americkay, judgin' by your manner o' speakin'."

"Well, yes, I *have* visited that country, Officer—for purely business reasons, you know."

"He's lying, he's lying, he's lying!" cried Laura, unable to contain herself any longer. "Oh, Constable, can't you *see* that he's Hiram P. Harper—he's just shaved his beard off, that's all, and dressed in different clothes. He and Mr. Smarmling and Miss Peach were trying to kidnap me and take me away as a hostage on the *Alabama,* and Miss Peach and Mr. Smarmling have stolen jewelry and silver from my house and packed it in a trunk, and they're going to run away abroad together, and they're hiding in the church right now and . . . and . . . oh, everything is so terrible and *why* won't you believe me and *do* something instead of writing everything down in that silly notebook?"

P. C. Crumble was desperately trying to scribble down everything that Laura was saying, but he put his pencil away when he heard her last remark, and looked slowly from Harper's sullen and shifty face to Laura's tear-stained and appealing blue eyes.

"Perhaps you're right, miss," he said, adding doubtfully, "Maybe I ought to flourish my truncheon?"

"Oh, please do, please do!" cried both Laura and Raymond together, whereupon the constable produced his weapon—a long black wooden object with several notches on the handle, twirled it in the air several times and said:

"John Smith, I arrest you on suspicion of being 'Iram P. 'Arper, alias 'Arpoon 'Arry, wanted for the murder of American Agent Roebuck, an' I warn you that anything you say—"

But Harper was no longer there. Wrenching himself free from

the constable's grip, he bounded over the churchyard wall, darted around a corner—and literally disappeared. Although they gave chase immediately, there was no sign of him when they came into the long empty street into which he had turned. On each side were the blank-looking doors and windows of respectable houses, behind which respectable people were just settling down to respectable helpings of Sunday roast beef. It was impossible that any of these doors could have opened to admit such a disreputable fugitive from justice as Harpoon Harry. Where, then, could he be? Constable Crumble removed his helmet to give his head a puzzled scratch. Mullinger sniffed around uncertainly. Laura looked ready to burst into tears again. Raymond said in a blank voice:

"It looks almost as if the street opened and ... and ... swallowed him up!"

"Exactly!" said Wally. "That's just what *did* 'appen! Raymond, me lad. You've 'it the nail on the 'ead!"

He pointed to a manhole in the middle of the street. The cover was sticking up slightly as if it had been dislodged and replaced in a hurry. Laura said slowly, with a slight shudder:

"Of course—the sewers. Well, we'll never catch him now. There are miles of those tunnels and hundreds of outlets. Father told me that some of the poor workfolk go down there trying to find things they might sell. That's probably what gave Harper the idea."

"There's still just a chance we might catch that dratted butler, though," said Wally, doubling back toward the church.

But the church was empty. The only sign of Smarmling's recent presence was a damp patch on the cold tiles, where he had sunk down perspiring after Raymond's charge. That and a piece of paper which must have fallen from Miss Peach's reticule as she fumbled in it for cologne or smelling salts to restore her deflated hero. It was Wally whose sharp eyes noticed the paper, which was folded up very primly into a small tight square. He unfolded it and read:

Messrs. Pickford's Fly Boats
Expeditious Water Conveyance from
Preston to Liverpool
(via Blackstone and Manchester)

RECEIVED from Miss PEACH the sum of TWO SHILLINGS, being the cost of conveying ONE TRUNK weighing a total of FIFTY-SIX POUNDS from BLACKSTONE to LIVERPOOL on WEDNESDAY 22nd JULY 1862. Trunk stored in chimney at Mr. Charles Hamilton's and to be collected therefrom by Messrs. Pickford's carrier on MONDAY 20th JULY.

"But which chimney?" cried Laura as she puzzled over this strange receipt. "There are at least twenty chimneys in our house. We shall have to search every one!"

"That," said Wally, "will be my pleasure, miss. I shall 'ave the honor of calling upon you professionally, suitably equipped and with trained assistants, first thing in the morning."

5

A CHASE UP
A CHIMNEY

*in which Mr. Wally's Climbing Boys make a merry
entrance, Laura and Raymond make a perilous as-
cent, and P. C. Crumble makes an important arrest.*

"There's a letter from the council," said Mrs. Price. "The new
flat will be ready in a few days. We'll have to think about
packing."

Raymond was scarcely listening. His head ached, his mouth
was dry, and his arm was painfully bruised where the doctor,
who had had to be called during the night, had been clumsy with
the injection. Mrs. Price looked at him anxiously. She wondered
again if she ought to ring the hospital, or at least try to arrange
for a day nurse to come in, but Raymond always got so upset
when she suggested these possibilities that the doctor had said
it was better to leave things as they were for the present.

"He's in no immediate danger—and he *has* even shown signs
of improvement recently. . . . Of course he has relapses too, but
it's too early to make any big decisions. The next week or so
might prove crucial. We'll leave him where he is for the time
being—he seems happy here at least."

Raymond had overheard the doctor talking to his mother, but
apart from vaguely wondering what words like "relapses" and
"crucial" meant, he took very little notice of what was said. He
was content to know that he was staying where he was and not

66

being fussed over by some busybody nurse who would prevent him from seeing his friends.

"Perhaps I'll call in today and make some inquiries," Mrs. Price went on. "We've really got so little stuff that it's hardly worth hiring a van. Perhaps Pickford's would be the best firm for the job. They're quite cheap at any rate."

Raymond pricked up his ears at the mention of Pickford's.

"Yes, I know," he said. "They only charge two shillings— that's . . . er . . . ten new pence—for half a hundredweight of goods. And that was from here to Liverpool."

Mrs. Price gave him a puzzled look.

"You do say some funny things, dear. I suppose your friend Laura told you that?"

"No. Actually it was Wally. He found this receipt, you see . . ."

"Yes, dear, I see. Well, now, you settle down and have a nice long rest to make up for your disturbed night. It won't be long now before you're up and about again and helping me to decorate the new flat."

Raymond closed his eyes obediently, and Mrs. Price got her lunch box ready, put on her coat and headscarf, and tiptoed out of the room.

It was seven thirty. The demolition men were already at work. Raymond could hear the great iron ball crashing into a wall, now only four or five houses away. They were a jolly lot, the demolition men—shouting to each other and singing and playing their transistors when they knocked off for tea breaks or lunch. They seemed to enjoy their work of destruction. One of them was passing along the street just now with a wheelbarrow of rubble, whistling cheerfully. He was followed by a gang of four or five very small boys—too small for Boy Scouts, almost too small for Cubs—whose faces, hands, and legs looked even blacker than those of the grimy workmen. They were marching along in military formation, singing a song, and—yes— accompanying their piping voices Raymond could hear the sweet and stirring tones of Wally's trumpet:

"Say, darkies, have you seen the massa
    with the mustache on his face
Go 'long the road some time this mornin',
    like he goin' to leave this place?
He seen the smoke, way up the river,
    where the Lincoln gunboats lay;
He took his hat and left very sudden,
    and I 'spect he's run away!"

Wally and the boys marched down the steps and into the basement, still singing at the tops of their voices. As he heard the chorus:

"The massa run? ha, ha!
The darky stay? ho, ho!
It must be now the kingdom comin'
And the year of Jubilo!"

Raymond thought for a moment that these must be little black slaves somehow brought over from America, but, looking more closely, he realized that their faces were black with *soot* and that what they were carrying over their shoulders were not hoes for chopping cotton but the extension handles of chimney sweeps' brushes. He also saw that Wally and each of the boys were wearing a large paper badge on which the letters "SACB" were prominently displayed. Mullinger was carrying a whole tray of these badges around his neck, as people do on flag days, and he had the collecting box strapped to his tail, so that it jingled as he wagged.

"Have a flag, sir," said Wally, pinning one on the lapel of Raymond's pajamas. "No charge to you, of course."

"What are they for?" asked Raymond.

"The Society for the Abolition of Climbing Boys," said Wally proudly. "I'm the honorary president of the Blackstone Branch—and here are five Climbing Boys who've just been abolished. Nick, Tim, Paddy, Chris, and Tom—step forward and meet my good friend Raymond."

The little boys, who were all smaller than Raymond, came forward rather shyly at first, but soon they began chatting away happily when Raymond asked them where they lived.

"We live up at Mr. Wally's place," said Nick.

"'E's got 'undreds of us up there," butted in Tim.

"Fousands, more like," corrected Paddy.

"'Undreds of fousands," added Chris.

Tom was just about to raise this to millions when Wally intervened. "I'm afraid the lads exaggerate a little. All the same, I 'ave a fair number. I've collected them over the years," he added vaguely.

"But if they don't climb any more, why are they so . . . grubby?"

"Oh, they *climb* all right! All boys climb. And they're grubby all right. All boys are grubby too. We don't 'ave no compulsory washin' up at my place. Just an occasional bath or shower. But the point is, they don't get shoved up *chimneys* no more. They 'elp me with the brushes and suchlike, and carry out minor investigations of the lower flues, but they don't get tortured or beaten or scorched on their bare feet or tickled wi' straws or pricked wi' knives to make 'em go 'igher and 'igher."

"An' we don't get our sore knees an' elbows rubbed wi' brine to 'arden the skin," said Nick.

"An' we don't 'ave to sleep in the soot sacks," added Tim.

"An' we get dinner every day, wiv puddin'," volunteered Paddy.

"Two or free 'elpins," nodded Chris.

"Six or seven if you want 'em," challenged Tom.

Wally again had to intervene as the discussion escalated. "Speakin' of food," he said, "it's time we 'ad a morsel of breakfast before startin' the day's work. Mrs. Porson, no doubt, will oblige."

Laura was in the kitchen with Mrs. Porson when Wally, Raymond, Mullinger, and the boys came around the screen. In spite of all her anxieties, she was rather enjoying being mistress of the household, especially now that Smarmling and Miss Peach were no longer there to order her about. Early that morning she had drawn up, with the help of a brand-new book called *The Book of Household Management* by Mrs. Isabella Beeton, a timetable for the main household events of each day. In her very best lettering, using only black crayon on white card (not a different color for each word or letter, which would have made it look a bit childish), she printed out two copies of the timetable, one for the servants' staircase and one for the kitchen. Mrs. Porson was looking rather doubtfully at the kitchen copy when Wally and his friends arrived.

Order of the Household

Morning Prayers .... 8.45 A.M.
"Not forsaking the assembling of ourselves together"

MEALS

Breakfast (kitchen and nursery)	8 AM
Breakfast (dining room)	8:30 AM
Kitchen dinner	12:30 PM
Luncheon	1:30 PM
Kitchen and nursery tea	5 PM
Dinner	6:30 PM
Kitchen supper	9 PM

Post arrives 8 AM
"Kind words in which we feel the pressure of a hand."
Post Departs 8:30 AM and 6 PM
"A timely written letter is a rivet in the chain of affection."
PLEASURES AND DUTIES IN DUE ORDER LINKED
Evening Prayers 10 PM

After some thought, Laura had added to the bottom of each notice the words:

"SINGED: Laura Frances Caroline Hamilton (Miss)

"I'm not sure as 'ow we can 'ave mornin' an' evenin' prayers with your father absent," said Mrs. Porson. "There'll be no one to lead 'em."

"I'll lead them," said Laura.

"No, miss, ladies ain't allowed to address the Almighty—leastways not in public."

"Perhaps Wally could do it. Could you, Wally?"

Wally looked rather alarmed. "I doubt it, miss. I mean, I wouldn't like to risk it. Me bein' such a little chap an' all—I doubt if my voice would carry that far."

"In that case," said Laura, feeling somewhat relieved, "we'll have to leave out the prayers."

"Very sensible, miss—but I 'ope we don't 'ave to leave out the breakfast," said Wally, winking at the boys and glancing up at the kitchen clock.

"Goodness," Laura said. "It's seven thirty already. Now, Cook, what shall we have?"

She quickly thumbed through Mrs. Beeton till she reached a page headed "Family Breakfasts for a Week in Summer."

"Ah, here we are. 'MONDAY: Poached eggs, grilled cutlets, bacon, potted beef, cold ham, stewed figs, fresh fruit in season, marmalade, jam, butter, dry toast, bread, fresh rolls, coffee, tea, hot and cold milk.' How does that seem?"

Mullinger licked his lips loudly, and the two smallest climbing boys began to dribble, causing white channels to appear in their sooty masks. Mrs. Porson, who seemed only just to have noticed the boys, looked at them sharply. Mullinger, sensing trouble, slunk away under the table.

"I 'ope, miss," said Mrs. Porson, "that I am not expected to feed these . . . these . . . urchins!"

"Indeed you are," replied Laura, feeling her position challenged.

"In that case, miss, I'm 'andin' in my notice!"

"Allow me to explain, ma'am," said Wally hastily. "These . . . er . . . these young lads are . . . er . . . so to speak, under my protection, and I'd take it as a personal favor, ma'am, if you could see your way to feedin' 'em."

Mrs. Porson's expression softened as Wally spoke, but she continued to eye the climbing boys with suspicion. At length she said:

"Dear Mr. Wally, a woman's 'eart is wax in the 'ands of a man like you." Here she touched her rather wobbling bosom as if to prove what she meant. "I can't refuse you anythin', you know I can't—but perhaps," (she added, blushing), "you'll do somethin' for me in exchange. . . . "

"Name it, ma'am," said Wally gallantly.

"Call me Gertrude!"

Wally gulped. Then, summoning up all his courage, he managed to blurt out "Gert," but his courage failed him when he tried to say the "rude" bit, and he ended up by converting it into a half-hearted splutter which made it sound more like "prune." But Mrs. Porson seemed satisfied and, giving Wally a playful tap with a huge frying pan, she proceeded to set before them a mammoth breakfast.

They had only just begun it (that is to say, they had only just had the poached eggs and grilled cutlets) when a housemaid arrived to say that there was a policeman at the door asking to speak to Miss Laura. Laura hurried away anxiously and returned a moment later with P. C. Crumble.

"The constable says that he has been assigned to watch the house in case Harpoon Harry makes any further attempt to kidnap me. So I've invited him to take his meals in the kitchen."

The cook nodded and began to lay the constable a place at the table next to the climbing boys, but he moved himself along until he was sitting next to her.

"Beg pardon, ma'am," he said, "but as a general rule I don't 'old with boys. Nasty creatures they are—allus in trouble with the law."

Mrs. Porson smiled in sympathy with this view. Encouraged by this, the constable went on:

"In fact, ma'am, I like to take my victuals as far away from boys as possible." He moved a little closer to Mrs. Porson. "But I don't mind saying that I appreciate the company of an 'andsome woman—especially if that woman knows as much about cookin' as you do, ma'am."

The very faintest tinge of a blush began to creep up from Mrs. Porson's bosom.

A gleam of hope lighted up in Wally's eye.

As soon as breakfast was over, Wally and the climbing boys went off to search the chimneys. Laura stayed behind in the kitchen to give orders for the day's meals and to help in the preparation of the soup and stew that were being made in huge vats for the hungry workfolk. Then she and Raymond went upstairs, wandering from room to room to see how the search was getting on.

Raymond enjoyed strolling through the house, stopped here and there to examine a curious ornament or to look at an embroidery or a painting. Nothing in the house (except Laura's nursery) was gay or bright—the furniture and woodwork were all dark brown, the curtains, carpets, and wallpapers all rich, deep colors—but everything seemed solid, comfortable, and safe. Most of the furniture had a round, cosy, tubby shape—even table legs and chair backs—so that, though they were dark and heavy, they never looked grim or ugly. Raymond thought that lots of the things looked rather like the statue of Queen Victoria that stood near the bus station—a bit dumpy, perhaps, and a bit too well padded, but sensible and settled and snug. Even though most of the rooms were deserted, except here and there for a housemaid polishing chair legs or dusting picture frames, the house seemed warm and lived in. It felt to Raymond like a house that was built to last forever.

One room especially he liked, and that was Laura's mother's room. It was a small room at the back of the house, overlooking the long walled garden. It was full of pictures, some of them painted by Mrs. Hamilton herself and some of them by famous artists whom she had known. They were not like the grand and rather solemn pictures in the rest of the house, which had titles like "Samson Among the Philistines" or "Queen Elizabeth Hears of the Defeat of the Armada." Those were quite interesting pictures, but once you'd looked at them for a little while they became boring because you could see exactly what they were telling you. But the pictures in Mrs. Hamilton's room were more mysterious, because every time you looked at them they seemed to tell a different story.

There was one picture, for instance, called "The Death of Roland." It showed the famous knight Roland standing on the top of a hill at Roncevalles, where his army had been ambushed and massacred by the Saracens. All around him lay the dead bodies of his companions, including his dear friend Oliver and the brave and holy Archbishop Turpin. Roland too was dying, but with his last breath he was blowing his great ivory horn to call the forces of Charlemagne to his assistance. The horn was the most splendid thing in the picture, more splendid even than the great sword Durendal that hung at Roland's side, and as he blew it, his face was shining with a strange light. It seemed as if this picture should have been sad—like the picture "The Death of Nelson" that hung in one of the downstairs rooms—but instead there was something exciting and jolly about it. And yet it was sad at the same time. That was the puzzling thing.

There were other nice things in Mrs. Hamilton's room too, especially her jewelry, which was set out in a tray on her dressing table just as it had been when she was alive. This had not been found by Smarmling or Miss Peach because the room was kept permanently locked, and only Laura and her father knew where to find the key. It was not expensive jewelry (the really expensive jewels had been locked away in Mr. Hamilton's study, from which Smarmling had taken them), but Raymond liked it because it was quaint and unusual. There was a bracelet made out of plaited strands of Mrs. Hamilton's own hair. It was a rich auburn color and fastened with a gold clasp. And there was a locket containing a single tiny curl which had been cut from Laura's head when she was a baby.

"Fancy being able to make a bracelet out of hair," mused Raymond.

"Lots of things can be made out of hair," Laura said. "Papa

told me that there was a vase made of it at the Great Exhibition."

"I wonder if *we* could plait something with it?" said Raymond.

"I'm sure we could," cried Laura enthusiastically, and seizing a dainty pair of scissors from her mother's dressing table she impulsively snipped off a long curling lump of her dark abundant hair.

Raymond had thick blond hair. One of the nice things about being ill was that his mother, who didn't really approve of long hair for boys, had let him grow it, so that it was now almost shoulder length. He too seized the scissors and cut off a long silky skein.

Sitting side by side on the little chaise longue, they each began to plait a neat ribbon of hair. Into Laura's plait went some of Raymond's golden hair, and into Raymond's went some of Laura's dark lustrous curls. When the two ribbons were complete, Laura twisted one into an R and one into an L, and laid the two letters side by side. Raymond looked at them for a moment and then placed them together like this:

Then he bound the two letters together firmly where they overlapped. There was still quite a lot of hair left. Laura quickly wove it into a new ribbon, which she twisted into the shape of a heart. Raymond then bound the initials into the heart, where they fitted neatly and snugly like this:

Neither of them spoke a word while they worked, and neither of them even looked at the other. Then Laura said:

"Let's put in it Mother's locket, and I'll wear it always and it will be our secret for ever and ever."

She took the large heart-shaped locket from her mother's tray and placed the hair-brooch inside it, where it lay glowing like a jewel against the dark velvet background. Then she strung the locket on a delicate golden chain, and Raymond fastened the clasp at the nape of her pretty little neck.

On their way back downstairs they met Wally and the climbing boys. Wally had a puzzled look on his face.

"It's a mighty funny thing, miss," he said. "We've checked every chimney in the 'ouse but there's no sign of any trunk."

"Are you *quite* sure?" cried Laura. "Oh, Wally, the trunk *must* be there somewhere, and we *must* find it!"

"It's strange," said Raymond in the baffled silence that followed, "that the receipt said 'chimney' without mentioning *which* chimney. It almost makes it sound as if Mr. Hamilton has only *one* chimney."

"And so he has!" cried Wally, with sudden inspiration. "Only one *mill* chimney! Raymond's figured it out again! What a lot of ninnies we've been! Come on—if we don't get there pretty slippy, we'll be too late!"

They raced away at full speed through the streets still crowded with aimlessly loitering workmen, forlorn little family groups, and tattered pale-faced children. Everywhere people looked drawn and thin. It was like running through a town of ghosts. Only in one part of the town was there any sign of cheerful, happy work. This was where a huge tract of uneven rocky ground was being transformed bit by bit into an ornamental park. All over Lancashire similar parks were being created, or reservoirs were being scooped out of the moorland rock, to provide work for thousands of idle hands. But alas, only a tiny fraction of these hands could be employed on these projects. For every five hundred men who pressed forward to dig ditches, level hills, or hew granite, only one could be given a job.

The rest prowled miserably around their little cottages, or wandered through the streets, or met together in schoolrooms to pass the time in teaching each other to read or write or study subjects which up to now only rich gentlemen had had enough leisure to study. But though they longed more than anything for the reopening of the mills, the busy clatter of the looms, and the cheerful companionship of their workmates in the hot and dusty spinning and weaving sheds, they continued to support Mr. Lincoln's blockade of Confederate cotton ports, because the sufferings of the poor black slaves in the cotton fields meant more to them than their own terrible trials.

As Raymond, Wally, and Laura entered the maze of narrow winding back streets dominated at intervals by the looming mills, Wally suddenly stopped and pointed ahead to a great mill which had just now come clearly into sight. Its huge chimney stack soared up 150 feet above the roofs of its highest blocks of buildings, and in bold white letters running down more than half the length of the chimney the name of the mill could be read: "Charles Hamilton."

Raymond and Laura almost laughed out loud at each other as they realized that this was obviously what the receipt meant by "the chimney at Mr. Charles Hamilton's." But Raymond also gave a little shudder and for a moment felt almost too dizzy to run when he got closer to the great towering chimney and noticed a steeplejack's ladder clinging like a flimsy ribbon to its side. Perhaps because he had lived all his life in a basement, Raymond couldn't stand heights. The thought that men actually had to work at the top of that chimney, clinging to that tiny thread of wood and iron, filled him with a sick, giddy horror.

But he had not much time to dwell on these thoughts, because they were already running across the mill yard toward the great gaping door of the boiler house. Inside this shed were the massive double doors of the iron furnace, which led into the base of the chimney. Of course the furnace had not been lighted for many months, and a strange eerie silence hung over the place. As the iron doors swung open, and they crept into the black mouth of the furnace, Raymond remembered the story of Ulysses and his men creeping into the cave of the one-eyed giant Polyphemus, and he shivered at the thought of what might be lurking there in the shadows.

Once inside, it took them some time to accustom their eyes to the darkness, but when they had done so, they could see that the bottom of the chimney was really like a huge room, with great broad shelves or ledges rising like steps up each side until they disappeared somewhere in the cavernous black hole above. These shelves were where most of the soot collected, and they rose up the chimney to a height of about twenty feet. Beyond that there were no more steps, but the sides of the chimney rose sheer and steep, with just a jutting fire brick and an iron rung at intervals of about a foot, forming a crude ladder for steeplejacks who had to inspect or repair the inside walls of the chimney.

The lower shelves had been swept clean of the soot that usually covered them to a depth of a foot or more, so it was quite easy for Wally, the children, and the boys to clamber from shelf to shelf in their eager search for the trunk. But though they went carefully along every ledge, feeling in the remotest corners and recesses, there was no sign of anything. Forlornly they scrambled down to the boiler floor and stared at each other in glum silence. Wally was the first to speak.

"Well," he said, "I could 'ave bet my bottom dollar that they'd be 'ere. But now we'll 'ave to put our thinkin' caps on and start all over again."

At that moment the iron doors of the boiler, which they had left ajar to give a little more light, closed behind them with a grim clang.

They heard the click of a pistol being cocked, and out of the shadows a voice spoke, a deep harsh American voice which froze their blood: "You certainly will have to think again, and you'll have to think fast. The trunk was sent on its way two hours ago. And now I intend to collect Miss Laura Hamilton and lock the rest of you in here until the mill reopens—which will not be until the *Alabama* sails."

Raymond and Laura were standing close together near the lowest ledge. He clutched her hand in the darkness and whispered, "Quick, follow me!" Before she realized what was happening, he was half pulling and half pushing her up from ledge to ledge until they had reached the topmost narrow ledge twenty feet above the floor of the boiler. From down below, the mocking voice of Harper called up:

"It ain't much use tryin' to escape that way—unless you can crawl up the walls like flies."

But Raymond had seen the steeplejacks' rungs and footholds. He whispered to Laura:

"Now listen carefully. These footholds lead to the top of the chimney. I'll go first, you follow. Don't look down and don't think about the height. Harper will come up the ledges to see where we are—and when he does, the others may be able to escape and get help. Be brave—it's our only chance!"

He put his arm around her, and for a moment they clung together in the darkness. Then they began to climb. Slowly and cautiously they inched their way up, from rung to foothold, from foothold to rung. Fortunately mill chimneys are built in such a way that the inside walls slope inward toward the base, so that for the first fifty yards or so it was more like climbing up a very steep sloping rock than up an absolutely vertical face. This gave them time to get used to the climb a little before the vertical part came. Another thing that helped them was the darkness. Even if they were tempted to glance down, it was impossible to see the bottom of the chimney, so they had no idea of the height they were reaching.

From time to time Raymond stopped and whispered back to Laura, "Don't be afraid. Follow me. It's safe as houses," and each time Laura's brave little voice came back: "I'm following, I'm not afraid."

Every time he came to a new rung or foothold, Raymond tested it carefully to make sure that it was firm. Once a rung began to come loose from the crumbling brickwork, and for a moment his head went dizzy, and he felt himself falling. His fingers clutched blindly at the wall and found a deep crack in the cement which served for a handhold. He clung to this crack until his fingers bled and then gradually edged his way up to the next rung. Then he dangled his free foot so that Laura could hold on to it while she too found the handhold in the cement.

So, bit by bit, they ascended until at last the increased light warned them that they were nearing the top of the chimney. Meanwhile, down below, Harper had become impatient after several minutes of waiting. Cursing angrily, he rammed a huge wooden wedge against the boiler door, jamming the handle so that Wally and the boys couldn't escape. Then he leaped from shelf to shelf in the lower flues of the chimney, trying in vain to find where the children were hiding. It was not till he got to the top ledge that he realized that the birds had flown, and, with a snarl of rage, he spotted for the first time the hand and footholds up the side of the chimney.

What was he to do now? For a moment he stood there irresolute, debating furiously with himself. Should he give chase and terrorize the children into coming down? Or should he wait at the bottom until sheer weariness and fatigue forced them to descend? After a moment's hesitation, he decided to go in pursuit, so clutching his pistol between his teeth he grabbed the first rung and began to climb.

He had no fear of heights. Having served in many a high-masted sailing ship, where he had scrambled up the ratlines to the crow's nest or out to the end of a slippery yardarm in howling gales, he was as agile and fearless as a cat. Even when the unsafe rung came away in his hand, he kept a cool head and a perfect balance as he sprang for the rung above. Very soon he could see the children toiling up ahead of him to the top of the chimney.

He called out to them, "Come back, you little fools, or I'll shoot," but though his voice behind them struck panic into their hearts, they continued climbing steadily.

Now Raymond was very close to the rim of the chimney, and a deep fear came over him. At what point on the rim would they emerge? Would it be on the same side of the chimney as the steeplejack's ladder, which he had noticed from the street? And even if it was, would he dare to clamber over the chimney's edge and onto that terrible ladder to begin the descent?

His first question was soon answered. As his head came up above the rim of the chimney into the vast and terrifying space of blue air, he saw at once that the ladder was at the opposite side of the huge circular ledge of brick on which he was now perched. He would have to work his way around that ledge, lying flat on his stomach and gazing down in sick horror at the factory roofs and cobbled yards so far, far below. The chimney rim was about two feet thick at its top edge and formed a circle about fifteen feet in diameter.

Pausing only to say to Laura, "Do exactly as I do and keep your eyes closed as you go around the rim," he got astride the brickwork, like a jockey astride a horse, leaning forward until he was flat and clutching it for dear life, his eyes screwed so tightly shut that his face ached with the effort. Then, inch by inch, he began to wriggle and squirm his way along.

Inch by inch, centimeter by centimeter. If he had been doing this on a wall in the park or the school playground, even a much narrower wall than this, he would have laughed at the thought of worming his way along so painfully and fearfully. Indeed, he would have done it standing up, probably even running, and for a dare he might even have hopped along it on one leg! But now the terrible thought of the vast emptiness gaping below him filled him with a sick fear that was worse than anything he had ever known, even in the worst moments of his long illness. It was only the thought of Laura that enabled him to go on at all—Laura, who was so sweet and so brave and who depended so much upon him to set her an example of courage and lead her to safety.

At last Raymond's groping hands felt the topmost rungs of the ladder. Now he had to slide his body over to the outer wall of the chimney and, still clinging with his arms to the rim, let his legs dangle in the void below until they found a secure foothold on the ladder. A high wind was whistling all around the top of the chimney, and he could hear the ladder rattling and clattering in the blast. What if it was not securely fixed? What if the steeple-jacks, who had finished repainting the huge letters on the wall, had already dismantled some of the clamps that held the ladder to the iron hoops? But there was no going back now. Harper was still a long way behind them, and their only hope was to maintain their lead.

Raymond called out to Laura, explaining what she had to do. Then he swung his body outward, and his legs dangled free, with 150 feet of nothingness between them and the ground. For one panic-striken moment, as his foot groped in the air, it seemed as if the ladder had disappeared, and he would have to hang there forever. Then his foot touched a rung, and he felt the uprights of the ladder between his hands, and he began to descend. Now he opened his eyes but kept them firmly fixed upward, where Laura too had just managed to edge herself over onto the ladder. Rung by rung they began to descend, and Raymond could measure their progress by glancing at the five-foot-high letters that ran down at the side of the ladder. Slowly but surely they edged their way down past the huge C, then the H, the A, the R. . . . Somehow the name of Laura's dear papa gave them new confidence, so much so that when Raymond had reached the letter L and Laura the letter R, Laura looked down to Raymond to call out something.

It was a disastrous mistake! Far, far below, the mill lay like the tiny blocks of her nursery building set, and all around the mill the whole town looked no bigger than a miniature model village seen through the wrong end of a telescope. Laura's bones turned to water. Her stomach heaved, and a cold sweat broke out over her whole body. She clung to the ladder in terror, her knuckles white and her forehead pressed against an iron rung.

A terrible longing came over her to fling herself from the ladder and dash herself to death on the stones below. Her body was rigid with fear. She dared not move a muscle, and yet not to move was more agonizing still. Looking at her stiffened body from below, Raymond knew at once what had happened, and he knew that he must act to save her from her paralyzing terror before Harper caught up with them. There was only one thing to do. He must go back to her and coax her to descend, as he had sometimes heard that firemen coax terrified people onto their ladders from the tops of burning buildings. So he moved up, until his feet were on the rung below hers, his body firmly pressed against her, and his lips against her cheek.

"Laura," he said, "listen to me. Forget what you saw down below. We are safe here together. I love you and you love me. Remember the brooch that we made in your mother's room—the brooch you are wearing now in your locket. That brooch will bring us luck. The same letters that we put into the brooch are written here on the chimney beside us—the letters R and L. They are the middle letters of your father's name, which means that he is watching over us just as your mother is. If you can overcome your fear, we shall soon find him again, and then we shall be with him for always. He needs us to help him, so be brave and we shall soon be back on firm ground."

Raymond's words worked. Laura's rigid body relaxed. She turned her head slightly toward him and brushed his lips with a little kiss. Then Raymond began to move down, and she followed him with new confidence. For the last hundred feet of the descent neither of them felt any fear at all. Their hearts were singing with joy, and they knew that, whatever dangers they still had to pass, nothing could ever really harm them as long as they were together.

No sooner had Laura and Raymond set foot on the ground than they found themselves surrounded by Wally and the climbing boys, who had managed to force Harper's wedge out of the boiler doors and make their escape. When Laura expressed surprise at seeing them free, Wally said:

"You're forgettin', miss, that escape is my business. It takes more than a wedge o' wood to keep Walter Wilberforce Tulliver in. But we've no time to talk about that at the moment. There's another little problem to be dealt with first."

He pointed to the chimney, where Harper was no more than halfway down the ladder.

"Quickly," cried Laura. "We must run! We've still time to get away!"

"Steady on, miss, steady on," said Wally. "The boys and I've worked out a better idea, 'aven't we, boys?"

The boys grinned and jumped up and down in excitement. Wally went on:

"I'll tell you what to do, miss. You and Raymond get goin' as fast as your legs will carry you, an' bring back our good friend P. C. Crumble. Tell 'im 'e'll need the fire brigade too. That should 'elp to get 'im 'ere a bit more quickly."

"But what about you?" asked Raymond anxiously. "You'll be in terrible danger if you stay here. Harper is armed, and he won't hesitate to shoot as soon as he gets down."

"You mean *if* he gets down," grinned Wally, winking at the boys. "But look sharp now, no time to waste!"

With some doubt in their hearts but trusting to Wally's good sense, which had never let them down yet, Raymond and Laura dashed away. This time Laura took one or two shortcuts which she knew from the mill to the house, so they arrived back in the kitchen in half the time their previous journey had taken.

P. C. Crumble was still there. He had taken off his helmet and unbuttoned his tunic, revealing a thick striped flannel shirt beneath. He had also removed his boots and one sock, which Mrs. Porson was darning as he sat comfortably in the fireside chair drinking coffee from a large pot decorated with a pattern of rambler roses. He jumped up somewhat guiltily when the children entered.

" 'Avin' bin patrollin' the streets of the neighbor'ood for the last two hours in the course of my dooty, miss, I wore a large 'ole in the stockin' of my right foot, which necessitated the attention of a skilled needlewoman."

Mrs. Porson cast her eyes down modestly at this compliment, while the constable went on:

"If you would like to hexamine the said foot, miss, you will observe a large blister developin' in the region of the 'eel."

He lifted his foot for her inspection. It was large, flat, and red, with tufts of ginger hair on the toes. It gave off a strong aroma. Laura drew back from it a little and said:

"Dear Constable Crumble, I'm sure your foot must be terribly sore. When we get back, I'll dress it for you with a linseed and carbolic plaster. But right now you *must* come with us to Papa's mill and bring the fire brigade, because Wally and the climbing boys are there, and Harpoon Harry is coming down the chimney, and he has a pistol and if we don't get there soon he'll shoot them all. . . ."

A look of official importance came into the constable's face. He buttoned his tunic, strapped on his helmet, and took from Mrs. Porson the sock which she had just finished darning.

"Thank you, ma'am," he said, as he buttoned his boot. "I 'ope to 'ave the pleasure of your company again very soon. But dooty calls and danger threatens—and when danger threatens, Cedric Crumble is not the man to 'ang back!"

He gave her a stiff bow, which was slightly spoiled when his large and protruding bottom nearly upset a pan of apple dumplings, and followed the children from the kitchen at what might be described as a swift plod. Mrs. Porson gazed at his retreating figure, and as the door closed Raymond thought he heard her murmuring to herself the word "Cedric!"

At first the constable wanted to report the matter to the sergeant, but Raymond and Laura pleaded with him so urgently that he agreed to go straight to the fire station. Once again the red engine with its polished brasses went dashing through the streets, with Laura and Raymond clinging excitedly to each other as it swerved around corners and dodged in and out of drays and hansom cabs. Constable Crumble was standing on the footboard ringing the great brass bell, and he would have cut a gallant and romantic figure had it not been for the apple dumpling stains on the seat of his trousers.

When at last they reached the yard of the Charles Hamilton mill, a strange sight met their eyes. The climbing boys had been at work busily removing the four lowest sections of the steeplejacks' ladder, so that Harper had been stopped in his descent at just about the point where he had reached the letter N of "Hamilton." Realizing that he could make no more progress downward, he had begun to work his way back upward, but just at the moment when he was approaching the final section of the ladder, Wally appeared on the rim of the chimney. The children held their breath in horror as they realized that he was actually *walking* around the rim. When he reached the top of the ladder, he produced a small saw from his knapsack and proceeded to saw through the ladder just below the point where the topmost clamps held it to the brickwork. As the saw cut through the last fibers of wood, the whole of the top section of the ladder swung loosely outward from the wall, making it impossible for Harper to complete his climb. He was trapped in the middle of the chimney and could escape neither up nor down!

Leaving the constable and the fire brigade to make the final arrest, Wally, the children, and the boys set off for home. Now that their ordeal was over, Raymond and Laura felt suddenly exhausted and walked along in silence, hand in hand. The boys, on the other hand, discussed the day's events excitedly.

"That was the 'ighest chimbley I've ever bin up," said Nick.

"You nivver went up it!" objected Tim.

" 'E went 'igher than wot you did," put in Paddy.

"That ain't sayin' much," countered Chris.

"I went 'igher than the lot of you," boasted Tom.

" 'Aven't you forgotten something?" said Wally. "Raymond and Laura were the only ones who *really* climbed it. How about singing the Song of the Climbing Boys in their honor?"

"Yes, yes," they all cried. "Hurrah for Laura and Raymond!" Wally raised his trumpet and began to play a tune that Raymond knew well, but the words that the boys sang were different from the ones he knew:

"On top of old Smokey
All covered in grime
With brushes and soot bags
The little boys climb.

"They climb in the darkness,
They climb in the night,
But far above Smokey
They come to the light—

"The light that is shining
Beyond the sad years—
Where poor little soot boys
Shall weep no more tears. . . ."

So they marched on, singing lustily in their shrill piping voices, and Raymond and Laura joined in the words as if they had known them all their lives.

It was not till they got to Laura's front door that they realized that Mullinger had been missing all morning, and what made them realize it was his sudden appearance as he came bounding toward them from the opposite end of the street. He was carrying something in his teeth, and he laid it at Laura's feet. She picked it up and turned pale with excitement.

"It's Papa's glove," she cried. "Mullinger must have discovered where he is!"

Mullinger's tail wagged vigorously, his tongue hung out, and he opened his mouth in a great squeaky yawn—a sure sign that he was impatient to get moving.

"All right, old friend," said Wally. "Lead on!"

Laura's fatigue disappeared completely as they hurried once more through the streets. Perhaps at last they were going to find Papa. At least he must be safe somewhere nearby if Mullinger had found his glove. Oh, if only they could find him and rescue him, everything would be all right again! He would easily know how to trace Smarmling and Miss Peach and recover the stolen jewels, and get in touch with the port of Liverpool authorities to prevent the *Alabama*'s sailing. Raymond too was filled with thoughts of seeing Mr. Hamilton. What would he look like? He imagined he would be tall, with slightly gray hair and perhaps a dark curly beard, a quiet gentle voice, and a kindly twinkle in his eyes. He wouldn't be the sort of grown-up who made children feel unimportant. He would listen carefully when you talked to him, and look at your drawings or your models when you wanted to show them to him, and take an interest in things like how many marbles you had or what kind of games you liked to play—instead of always saying, "Go away, I'm too busy!"

But where was Mullinger leading them? They passed through the center of the town, across the main railway bridge and down beyond the back of the sidings and yards. Running parallel with the railway track in the remotest sidings was the canal, along which the barges brought huge bales of raw cotton from Liverpool, or took away the beautifully finished fabrics when they finally left the mills. Laura and Raymond looked at each other in consternation when they saw the black sluggish ribbon of water overhung by tall gloomy warehouses. Both of them had heard from time to time of bodies found floating in that murky water—bodies of children who had tumbled in while playing on the tow path, or bodies of desperate men and women who had committed suicide, or even, occasionally, bodies of people who had disappeared in mysterious circumstances and whose deaths were due to what the police called foul play. Could it be that Mr. Hamilton had been a victim of foul play? Was Mullinger leading them to a bloated and disfigured corpse floating face downward in the slime and scum that collected in the spiky reeds at the edge of that stagnant and motionless river?

But instead of taking the turn that led down to the towpath, Mullinger kept right on to the farthest siding, where a solitary freight train was stationed. It had an engine and tender, six cars and a caboose. The engine had a long tank with a high narrow chimney and a squat dome. The driver's cab was open, with just a weatherboard at the front to protect him from the head wind. Instead of the usual smart greens or reds with bright linings and polished brass or metal work, the whole engine and tender were painted dead black. The only thing that relieved the ugly drabness of the engine was its name, picked out in green letters on a brass plate on the side of the cab.

Being a railway enthusiast, Raymond was delighted with the engine. He wished he had his train-spotting book with him, so that he could note down its name, "*Vulcan*," and its number, *336*. Then he could look up its type and class and discover what its special features were. One thing he noticed was the peculiar shape of the dome over the firebox. Could that be the famous "cottage-loaf" design, which he knew that some of the old engines had had? He longed to jump into the cab and examine the controls—but already the others had followed Mullinger right along the train till he reached the caboose, where he began leaping up and down and wagging his tail in excitement.

The caboose was heavily bolted and padlocked, but on each side there was an iron-barred grille that served as a window. Laura and Raymond scrambled up to this grille together and peered eagerly inside. One thing was certain—Mr. Hamilton was not there! But his traveling cloak and hat were, and a large chest which Laura recognized as his traveling trunk, and a valise marked with his initials. There was also one glove lying beside the valise—the twin of the one which Mullinger had brought.

Obviously the train was going to be used to take Mr. Hamilton to Liverpool. The things he would need for the journey had been placed there in readiness—probably packed by Smarmling on the instructions of Grimskull and Harper—but whoever had brought them had dropped the glove, which gave Mullinger the scent. Though Laura was nearly weeping with disappointment at not finding her papa, she cheered up somewhat when Wally said:

"Look 'ere, miss, there's no need to take on so. This is a lucky find. For one thing it proves they don't intend to 'arm your papa.

They ain't treatin' 'im like a common prisoner—more like a gentleman 'ostage, allowin' 'im to take along 'is trunk an' travelin' clothes. But the best of it is that we now know 'ow they're intendin' to smuggle 'im away, so we can make one or two little plans of our own. Now, miss, if you leave everythin' to me, I'll 'ave a plan of campaign worked out by tomorrow mornin'—but just now I think we all need to go 'ome and get a bit o' rest. The next few days are goin' to be a bit 'ectic."

"But," cried Laura, "we can't just go home without leaving Papa a sign—something to tell him that we've been here and that we will come to his help!"

She took a red ribbon from her hair and tied it in the form of a bow. Then, glancing at Raymond, who nodded in agreement, she unclasped her locket and tossed both locket and ribbon through the iron bars of the grille, where they fell into a fold of the traveling cloak, nestling there like a tiny scarlet and golden flower in the cranny of a wall.

Somehow both Laura and Raymond knew, as they went sadly away from that grim black train, that their locket, which was the most precious thing in the world to them, was the best thing to leave behind as a sign of their love for Mr. Hamilton.

6
TRIAL AND ERROR

in which Hiram P. Harper goes before the magistrates, P. C. Crumble's pride goes before a fall, and Wally makes plans to go to Manchester before Mr. Smarmling.

"Pickford's will be calling to collect a few things today," said Mrs. Price. "No furniture yet, of course—just these two trunks of clothes, bed linen, and odds and ends which can go on in advance."

"Have you packed my railway books?"

"Well, yes, dear, I'm afraid I have. And your train set. You haven't asked for them for a long time."

"I just wanted to look something up, that's all. Can you just write down 'Number Three hundred thirty-six Vulcan' before I forget it?"

"Is that a new train number?"

"No, it's an *old* train number. I spotted it yesterday in the sidings over at the back of Central Station."

Mrs. Price smiled but looked worried. The doctor had warned her that Raymond might become a little delirious at times, but now it seemed that the delirium was becoming almost continuous. And there were other worrying things too. For instance, Raymond's hand was badly cut and scarred all across the fingers and knuckles. She had noticed it when she had given him his sponge bath, but he had not said anything about it so she didn't like to press him for an explanation. He certainly couldn't have been out of bed—he was much too weak even to sit up for very long without assistance—and Mrs. Nuttall, who came in more often now that Raymond needed so much more nursing, reported that Raymond always seemed to be dozing quite peacefully whenever she looked in. It was strange, too, that in spite of his rambling talk, he seemed just as bright and intelligent as ever in other ways. For instance, Mrs. Price had happened to mention that they were dismantling the chimney at her mill, since modern oil and electrical power made the old furnaces and chimneys useless, and Raymond had surprised her by describing in detail the design of the inside of the old mill chimneys.

Another thing that worried Mrs. Price was Raymond's attitude toward the new flat. It was a nice flat, in a pleasant suburb of the town. Raymond would have his own bedroom, and Mrs. Price for the first time in her life would have a properly fitted-out kitchen. Raymond seemed pleased about it for her sake but not really interested for himself. In fact most of the time he talked as if he weren't going to be moving at all—even though the demolition team was getting nearer every day.

But Mrs. Price fortunately had very little time to dwell on these thoughts as she bustled around getting herself ready for work. And there was one thing to be thankful for—Raymond never complained these days of being lonely or bored at home. He'd stopped asking when she would be able to get the television mended, and he hardly ever listened to the little transistor radio which she had borrowed for him. He seemed to be quite content with his own thoughts and fancies.

This morning, however, as she left for work, he did seem to be listening to the radio with more interest than usual. There was a news item about a hijacked airliner, and another one about a British diplomat who was being held as a hostage in a foreign capital.

"Mummy, why do people take hostages?" he asked.

"It's a way of forcing other people to do things. If they don't do them, the hostages get shot."

"Do they always shoot the hostages?"

"No. Sometimes they're just bluffing. But these days they usually carry out their threats. I don't know what the world's coming to, I'm sure, with all this violence."

As she closed the door, the news bulletin ended, and the usual early-morning record requests continued. Raymond was just about to switch off, when he heard a nice jazz number coming through, a gentle, playful tune with trumpet, trombone, and clarinet all weaving in and out of each other against the steady beat of the double bass and the *plunkety-plunk* of the banjo. After the first few bars, the record faded down, and the disk jockey's voice said:

"This request is from Wally, Laura, and all the climbing boys—sounds like a nice name for a mountaineering club—and is for Raymond Price, of Seventy-two King's Road, Blackstone, Lancashire. Raymond, your friends tell me you're quite a climber yourself, so here's a number you might enjoy—it's Mr. Acker Bilk and his Paramount Jazz Band playing their version of that lovely old song, "Higher Ground.""

Raymond could hardly believe his ears. Fancy him being named on the radio! How nice of Wally and Laura to think of it! And what a pity Mother wasn't there to hear it! He listened delightedly as the jazzmen tossed the tune from one instrument to another. Then the husky humorous voice of Mr. Acker Bilk came in with the lyric:

> "I have no desire to stay
> Where doubts arise and fears dismay,
> For I have caught a joyful sound—
> The song of Saints on Higher Ground.
>
> "Oh, lift me up, yes, let me stand
> By grace on Heaven's stable land—
> Higher plane than I have found,
> Lord, plant my feet on Higher Ground. . . . "

As the voice faded and the trumpet took the lead, Raymond was somehow not at all surprised to find that Wally had entered the room and was playing the trumpet part, using the mute to make it sound funny and wistful at the same time, just as the trumpeter had been doing on the record. Raymond beamed at Wally:

"Oh, thank you, thank you! That was such a nice surprise. But how did you get them to play your request so quickly? I thought you had to wait weeks or months."

"Oh," said Wally vaguely, "I've been on the air myself . . . and I've got . . . well, you know, connections."

Before Raymond could press for more details about these mysterious connections, Wally had slipped behind the screen. A moment later he reappeared, grinning all over his face.

"If you want to hear how P. C. Crumble arrested a desperate criminal single-handed and in the face of great danger, just step into the kitchen. The Saga is just about to begin!"

P. C. Crumble was seated at the kitchen table with a large breakfast before him. Beside him hovered Mrs. Porson and nearby stood Clara and Hannah, the kitchenmaids, Lizzie and Nelly, the housemaids, Philomena, the Irish parlor maid, and Sadie and Mary Ellen, the chambermaids. All were listening with rapt attention as the constable unfolded his story between mouthfuls of spiced brisket of beef and veal and ham croquettes.

"On arrival at the mill yard, I observed that 'Arper was 'eavily armed. 'E 'ad a shotgun in one 'and and a pistol in the other. 'E also 'ad a pistol between 'is teeth."

"Glory be to God," said Philomena, "and how did he come to be clinging to the ladder at all?"

The constable took a large mouthful of brisket while he considered this question. Then he went on:

" 'E'd 'itched 'imself on to it, miss—by 'is coattails. Cool as a cucumber, 'e was, but 'is eyes was blazin' with 'atred. I sez to myself, Crumble, there's murder in them eyes. That man's killed before an' 'e's prepared to kill again, I sez."

"But you surely couldn't see his eyes, and him halfway up the chimney?" said the incredulous Philomena.

Mrs. Porson gave her a withering look. "Don't interrupt the

constable," she said tartly, "or I'll oblige you to leave my kitchen!"

The constable, however, was unabashed by Philomena's question. "Police officers, miss, 'ave unusual eyesight. Take my eyes, for instance," he said, fixing her with a long fishlike stare. "You wouldn't think there was anything special about these eyes, would you now?"

"They stick out a bit," said Philomena.

"They're a funny color," added Nelly. "Kind o' pale green with pink edges."

"And they 'aven't got no proper eyelashes," ventured Clara.

The constable chose to ignore these unflattering comments.

"These eyes," he said, narrowing them to what he considered to be pinpoints, "can spot a suspicious movement at three 'undred paces. The moment I saw 'Arper up that ladder, my suspicions was aroused. I knew I 'ad to take immediate action. There wasn't a moment to be lost."

"What did you do?" asked Lizzie breathlessly.

"Did you challenge him to come down?" said Mary Ellen.

"No, miss, I did not."

"Did you shoot it out with him?" said Sadie.

"No, miss, I did not."

"Did you climb up alone and tackle 'im?" asked Hannah excitedly.

"No, miss, I did not."

"Oh, do tell us what you did," they all cried in chorus.

The constable paused to swill down the last mouthful of veal and ham with a long swig of coffee. Then he said impressively:

"I squirted 'im."

"Jesus, Mary, and Joseph!" cried Philomena. "And with what did you squirt him, Constable, may I ask?"

"I squirted 'im with my 'ose pipe," said the constable.

Philomena giggled, and the rest of the girls looked puzzled, so he added by way of explanation:

"I 'ad, of course, 'ad the presence of mind to bring the fire brigade along with me, just in case I might need a little assistance."

The girls looked at him admiringly. Mrs. Porson refilled his coffee mug and placed the toast and marmalade within his reach. He buttered himself a thick slice and continued:

" 'Tis no easy task to squirt a man at a distance of a 'undred feet or more. It calls for a keen eye and a steady 'and. But I were right on target with me first shot, an' I gave 'im a fair sousin'. Before 'e finally yelled out to be brought down, 'e were damn near drownded—if you'll pardon the expression, ma'am."

Mrs. Porson pardoned the expression with an indulgent smile and said:

"But I expect 'e still 'ad plenty of fight left in 'im when you got 'im down—a desperate criminal like that. No doubt you 'ad a bit of a job to overpower 'im, Constable?"

"That, ma'am, is puttin' it mildly. Fought like a tiger, 'e did—an' fought dirty too, like all these furriners. But I've done a bit o' wrestlin' in me time—Westmoreland style, you know, ma'am—so I quickly pinned 'im in the old 'alf-nelson, bopped 'im one wi' me truncheon and snapped the bracelets on 'im. Which reminds me, ma'am, may I borrow your carving knife for a moment?"

With some trepidation Mrs. Porson handed him a large carving knife with a curved whalebone handle. The girls backed away in alarm. Philomena made the sign of the cross. The constable brandished the knife professionally, took out his truncheon, and carved a deep notch on the handle. The girls looked relieved and gathered around to examine the truncheon.

"Just look at the number of notches 'e's got already," said Clara. "Tell us what they're all for, Constable."

P. C. Crumble placed the truncheon before him on the table and pushed his chair back a little. His right arm stole around Clara's waist and his left arm around Philomena's. An arch look came into his eye.

"Well," he said, "I'm a modest man an' I don't like to boast o' me exploits—but I might be persuaded to tell you if you'll sit on me knee."

Mrs. Porson's face darkened. She snatched up the truncheon as if it were a rolling pin and twirled it before the constable's face.

"Exploits indeed!" she snapped. "This is a respectable kitchen an' we'll 'ave none o' *those* kind of exploits 'ere! Off with you, you brazen little 'ussies! Get back to your jobs or t'master'll 'ear about this when 'e comes back."

The girls fled in alarm, and Mrs. Porson slammed the kitchen door behind them. A moment later it reopened, and Philomena's saucy face reappeared. "You'd best be watching out, Constable," she called. "I'm after thinkin' you'd be safer with two of us on your knee than with one of her."

Before Mrs. Porson had time to reply, Wally and Raymond stepped forward from the large cupboard by the side of which they had been observing the scene. Mullinger followed them, walking with a peculiar sideways gait to conceal the ham bone which he had just hooked from a low shelf.

"Good mornin' to you, ma'am," said Wally cheerily, pretending not to notice the fact that Mrs. Porson was perspiring heavily and brandishing a truncheon. "And a very good mornin' to you too, Constable. I trust our little affair of yesterday was successfully concluded. How did the actual arrest take place?"

"On arrival at the mill yard," began the constable, "I observed . . ."

"Ah, yes," said Wally, "and no doubt your observation was correct, Officer. The police are noted for the sharpness of their observation. But what was the *outcome* of your observation? In short, is our friend 'Arpoon 'Arry safely in jail—and when will 'e be brought to trial?"

" 'E's locked up in the police station at the moment, sir," said the constable, "and 'e's due to appear before the magistrates at eleven A.M. this very mornin'."

"In that case," said Laura, who had just appeared at the

kitchen door, "we had better make haste to be present there. No doubt we shall all be needed to give evidence."

The town hall, where the courts were held, stood in the middle of the large central town square. It was a huge building, a proud building, a brutal building. Its style was Gothic, like the cathedrals and castles of the Middle Ages, but all the grace and elegance of those lovely old buildings was missing. Instead of soaring lightly and superbly toward the sky, the towers of the town hall seemed to bear down heavily on the earth. Instead of glowing with mysterious beauty, its stained-glass windows seemed to glare with harsh ugliness. Instead of being a sign of comfort and safety and sanctuary for the poor and the weak, its spires and turrets seemed to be only a sign of the pride and dominance of the rich and the powerful.

Wally and the children arrived early, and the first court of the morning was still in session. There were two magistrates on the bench—Mr. Digweed and Mr. Record. Mr. Digweed was small and fussy, with a pale face, pink eyes, and furry white side-whiskers. He reminded Raymond of a hamster. Mr. Record was long and bony, with a blue chin, a bald head, and a beaky nose. He reminded Raymond of a vulture. As the children crept into their seats at the back of the courtroom, the police sergeant led into the dock a small boy of about Raymond's age. His face was pinched and furtive, and his clothes were hanging off him in ribbons. The magistrates' clerk read out the charge:

"Sam Clegg, you are charged with sleeping out in the dustbins behind the Puff and Dart public house on the night of the nineteenth of July. How do you plead?"

Since Sam Clegg said nothing, the sergeant answered for him: " 'E pleads not guilty, sir."

"Proceed with the evidence, Sergeant," said little Mr. Digweed in a light-colored voice.

The sergeant said that Sam Clegg was a persistent sleeper-out. He was a hardened case. He had been committed to prison on seven previous occasions for sleeping out, but he continued to sleep out. He was, however, extremely cunning, which made his crimes very difficult to detect. Instead of sleeping out in obvious places like shop doors or park benches, he craftily chose places which were not easily detected by policemen on the beat. He had been known to sleep out in sewers, in railway sidings, and in dog kennels, but his recent offenses had been committed behind the Puff and Dart public house, where, by concealing himself in a refuse bin, he had attempted to avoid detection.

A police constable corroborated the sergeant's statement and gave evidence of the arrest. Sam was then put in the witness box and questioned by the sergeant:

"Did you or did you not sleep out behind the Puff and Dart on the night of the ninth of July?"

"Well, no, I weren't exackly *out*."

"Come, come," said Mr. Record testily, "either you were in or you were out. Which was it?"

"It were both, sir."

"Both!"

"Yessir. Me top 'alf were out, sir, but me bottom 'alf were in t'dustbin."

"And do you consider a dustbin a respectable place to sleep?" asked Mr. Digweed, glaring severely over his spectacles.

"No, sir."

"Then why do you sleep there?"

"I 'aven't got no 'ome, sir. I'm an orflin'."

"But surely a boy of your age can find some useful work to provide yourself with a respectable shelter."

"I used to be a short-timer in t' mill, sir. But there's nowt to do there now, sir."

"Thrift," said Mr. Digweed sternly, "and self-help, and diligence are qualities by which man or boy can learn to survive even in the most difficult times of trial. In this great nation, built up by the thrift, self-help, and diligence of its respectable citizens, there is no place for the idler or the parasite. We sentence you to a fine of three guineas, or alternatively six weeks in prison. Which do you choose?"

Sam grinned ruefully. "Since I 'aven't got three 'a-pence, let alone three guineas, I reckon I choose prison, yer honor."

"But I reckon different," said Wally, suddenly standing up at the back of the court. "With your permission, yer honors, the fine will be paid by me."

Mr. Digweed dropped the wooden hammer with which he was about to rap the table to call for the next case. Mr. Record, who had nodded off during Mr. Digweed's final speech, came to life with a start. The clerk to the court made a huge blot on the page on which he was writing. The sergeant nipped his own thumb in the handcuffs which he was about to snap on Sam's wrists. Sam himself gazed around in wonder, as did everyone else, to see who had spoken.

Wally came forward and placed three golden guineas on the clerk's desk. Mr. Digweed peered at him suspiciously.

"May I inquire what is the reason for this unusual and unnecessary intervention?"

"I 'ave a . . . er . . . a sort of place for young fellers like this," said Wally vaguely.

"Do you mean to say you are the governor of an orphange?"

"Well, not exactly . . . no."

"Perhaps then you are the principal of a ragged school?"

"No, I wouldn't say that either. Schoolmasterin' isn't in my line."

"What, then, *is* your line?"

"I'm a chimney sweep."

The puzzled expression left Mr. Digweed's face. "Ah, now I see. You are seeking apprentices for your trade?"

"In a manner of speakin', yes," said Wally, and taking the bewildered Sam by the hand he returned to his place at the back of the court.

The next case was a boy of seven, charged with being a pickpocket. He was found guilty and sentenced to six months' imprisonment or a fine of five pounds. Wally produced the five pounds and added the little pickpocket to his collection. In this way, by the end of the session he had acquired a motley bunch of diminutive thieves, vagrants, vandals, rogues, rascals, and ragamuffins—not one of them more than ten years old. There were so many of them that they filled more than four rows of benches in the courtroom, so that in the end the criminals outnumbered the respectable citizens. Mr. Digweed, who was getting nervous, decided to bring the session to a close.

Before the court was cleared, the clerk announced that the next session would commence in ten minutes' time and that the presiding magistrate for that session would be Mr. Enoch Grimskull, assisted by Mr. Murgatroyd Grooch and Mr. Ezekiel Spurge!

"The court will rise. Silence in the court!"

As the three magistrates entered the courtroom, Raymond and Laura craned their necks to get a glimpse of them. Grimskull they already knew. His great craggy head and sunken eyes looked even harsher in daylight than they had looked at night. Grooch was a squat, square man, something like a frog, with a fat, flat head jammed straight onto his body, and no neck. Spurge was a small simpering man with very light blue eyes that seemed to look in different directions, so that you could never tell when he was watching you—although he always was. They took their seats in silence, and Harper was led in.

Since he had not shaved since his arrest, his heavy dark beard was already beginning to grow, and he looked unmistakably like the portrait in the police station. He was handcuffed between two policemen, and P. C. Crumble followed close behind with a proprietary air. The courtroom was packed, since the news of the arrest of a murderer had spread like wildfire through the town. Even the galleries were filled to overflowing, and crowds of people, mostly unemployed workers, had gathered outside on the town-hall square to await the verdict. Word had also got around that the accused man was a Confederate agent, so little sympathy was felt for him among the silent groups of half-starved workfolk in the square.

The charge was read out by the clerk

"Hiram P. Harper, you stand accused of the crime of murder, in that you did, on the twenty-seventh of May, 1862, willfully and with deliberate malice aforethought, kill Henry J. Roebuck, an agent of the United States Government, and dispose of his body in the River Mersey, from which it was recovered by the Liverpool river police on the fifth of June. Do you plead guilty or not guilty?"

"My client pleads not guilty."

The speaker was a large rubicund barrister with a purple knobbly nose on which were clipped a pair of rimless spectacles. He had flabby lips and a juicy, crackling kind of voice. His head was so bald that his wig had slipped down over his forehead, where it was prevented from slipping any further by a pair of beetling bushy eyebrows. He was Mr. Cyrus Grubb, Queen's Counsel, the senior member of the firm of Wagstaff, Wagstaff, and Grubb, of Paternoster Row, London.

A report from the Liverpool police, giving further details of the murder of Lieutenant Roebuck, was read to the court. P. C. Crumble was then called to the witness-box to give details of the actual arrest. He produced his notebook, took a deep breath and began:

"On Monday, the twentieth of July, I was called to the Charles 'Amilton Mill where I saw the accused, 'Iram P. 'Arper . . . "

"Objection, your honors," crackled Mr. Grubb.

"What is your objection?" asked Grimskull.

"The constable states that the accused man is Hiram P. Harper. But this fact has not yet been proved. I am prepared to maintain that this is a case of mistaken identity. The name of the man standing in the dock is John Smith. Unless the police can prove beyond doubt that he is Hiram P. Harper, I shall demand that the case against him be dismissed. I ask the court's permission to call witnesses who are prepared to give evidence as to the true identity of the accused."

"Objection sustained," said Grimskull. "You may call your witness before the constable proceeds any further."

Mr. Grubb then called to the witness-box a series of shifty-eyed and disreputable-looking characters, each of whom swore that the man in the dock was John Smith, that they had known the same John Smith for years, that he was a respectable grocer from Brondesbury in London, that he regularly traveled to Blackstone on business, and that it was ridiculous that he should have been mistaken for a notorious American wanted for murder. At length, when the last witness had given his testimony, Grimskull asked the constable if he had any statement to make in reply.

The constable's mouth dropped open in consternation. Having been cut short in his well-rehearsed story, he didn't quite know what to do next. He realized dimly that what he was being asked to do was to prove that Harper was Harper. But the more he thought about it the more puzzling that request seemed to be. How did you go about *proving* something that was quite obvious to see? It was like being asked to prove that Grimskull was Grimskull, or for that matter that Crumble was Crumble. In fact, *was* Crumble Crumble? After the amazing evidence he had just heard, he was beginning to doubt whether anybody was anybody. So confused was he that he never even thought of calling Wally and the children as witnesses. Instead, he returned to his notebook and began reading from it again where he had left off.

"... I saw the accused, 'Iram P. 'Arper ... "

"Objection," came again the inexorable voice of Mr. Grubb.

"Objection sustained," drawled Grimskull, and then, leaning forward across the high magistrates' bench, he said, "What led you to believe that the man you arrested was the wanted murderer?"

The constable floundered again for a moment and then managed to splutter, " 'E *looked* like 'im—in fact 'e was the spittin' image of 'im—all except the beard."

"Objection. The constable claims that the man he arrested looked like Harper. But the constable had never *seen* Harper. The most he had seen, perhaps, was a picture of Harper."

"Objection sustained," said Grimskull mechanically. "The

constable may, if he wishes, produce a picture of Harper for the court to inspect."

"I can't exactly prodooce one," said Crumble, "but there's one pinned up on the police-station wall, right between the notice about swine disease and the extracts from the Cock Fighting, Badger- and Bear-Baiting Act of 1835."

This last piece of information he brought out with a flourish, feeling confident that such a display of legal knowledge would convince even the mighty Mr. Grubb, Q.C., that he knew what he was talking about. But Mr. Grubb merely said:

"Objection. Evidence not produced in the courtroom cannot be accepted as evidence."

"Objection sustained," assented Grimskull.

The constable looked blank again. Then he had an inspiration. "Why don't you just ask 'im if 'e's Arper. Put 'im on 'is Bible oath and ask 'im. 'E won't be able to deny it. You can tell 'e's a Yankee as soon as 'e opens 'is mouth!"

"Unfortunately, your honors," said Mr. Grubb, "my client has lost his voice as a result of a drenching which he received in the course of his brutal handling by the police. However, I have no objection to his taking the oath. He may indicate his answers by a nod or a shake of the head."

Harper went to the witness stand and put his hand on the Bible while the oath was read to him. He nodded his acceptance of it.

"Your witness, constable," said Mr. Grimskull.

The constable had never before been invited to interrogate a witness. He felt that this was an important moment in his career, a moment when he could wipe out the rather foolish impression he had made so far in this trial. He adjusted his tunic, drew himself up to his full height, and fixed Harper with a glassy stare that was intended to mesmerize him:

" 'Iram P. 'Arper," he began impressively, forgetting for a moment that this was the very thing he was trying to prove, " 'Iram P. 'Arper, are you or are you not . . . 'Iram P. 'Arper?"

Though he still felt there was something wrong in the way he had phrased the question, he was confident of success. He could hardly believe his eyes, therefore, when Harper stared back at him with a cool and mocking look, and slowly and deliberately shook his head. Grimskull rapped the table with his wooden hammer.

"Case dismissed," he said briskly. "The accused is free to leave."

Before the children and Wally had time to realize what was happening or to raise an objection, Harper had swaggered out of the court, arm in arm with Mr. Cyrus Grubb. For a moment there was a stunned silence in the room. Then pandemonium broke out. People began booing and whistling at the magistrates. Somebody started a slow handclap, which turned into a chant of "We want justice, we want justice!" The chant was taken up by the waiting crowds in the square below, who had just seen Harper whisked away in Mr. Grubb's private carriage.

Grimskull was beside himself with fury. He brought the wooden hammer down on the table with such force that the head broke off.

"Silence in the court!" he yelled.

From somewhere suspiciously near where Sam Clegg was sitting, a rotten egg rose into the air, sailed through the courtroom, and landed with a sickly splat on Grimskull's bald cranium. It was followed by a moldy Brussels sprout which hit Spurge on the right ear and an evil-smelling codfish which smacked against Grooch's bulging double chin and slithered down under his waistcoat. There was a roar of laughter, and a voice piped up:

"Good shot, Sam, you've got yer 'at trick!"

The three magistrates were hustled under police protection into a room at the back of the court, and the people surged out onto the square. There they hung around in groups, talking over the events of the morning, too fatigued and listless to trek home to their bare cottages and foodless cupboards. After a little while, though, since Lancashire folk can never stay angry or sad for very long, one or two of the young mill girls started to dance on the square, and a young man called out:

"Come on, lads, join in. We might as well 'ave a bit o' fun, especially since its rush-bearin' time!"

Soon all the young folk were dancing while the older ones clapped an accompaniment or joined in the choruses of the cotton-mill songs:

> "I worked in a cotton mill all my life
> And I ain't got nothin but a Barlow knife,
> It's hard times the cotton-mill girls,
> It's hard times everywhere.

> "Us kids worked ten hours a day
> And got six bob of measly pay,
> It's hard times the cotton-mill girls,
> It's hard times everywhere.

> "When I die don't bury me at all,
> Just hang me up on the spinning-room wall
> And pickle my bones in alcohol,
> It's hard times everywhere."

Raymond and Laura and the sleepers-out, urchins, and ragamuffins joined in too, while Wally kept the tunes going on the trumpet and Mullinger—but where *was* Mullinger? It wasn't until the dancers and singers had begun to tire and the crowd had thinned out to just a handful that Wally realized Mullinger was missing. He had just said, "Drat that dog, I expect 'e's in love again!" when Mullinger appeared at the far side of the square, attentively paying court to a tiny black-and-white dachshund.

Before Wally had time to whistle, the dachshund disappeared down a side street, giving a cock of her leg and a flounce of her tail, which Mullinger seemed to take as a sign that he was

permitted to follow her. Wally and Laura and Raymond set off in
pursuit, Wally remarking:

"I don't mind Mullinger 'avin' a lady friend now and again,
but 'e does make such unsuitable choices! Last year 'e fell in love
with a Pekinese no bigger than a pennyworth o' tripe. An' before
that 'e 'ad 'is 'eart set on a Japanese toy spaniel called Kutzi-
Tuvi, that 'e could 'ave eaten in 'alf a mouthful. I think dogs is
like people," he added with considerable feeling. "They ought to
be matched up with someone their own size."

But there was no time for further reflections, since Mullinger
and his miniature girl friend had increased their pace and were
already about to disappear around another corner into a street
lined with warehouses. When Wally and the children themselves rounded the corner, the dogs had vanished, but an open
hatch in a large warehouse door showed where they had gone.
Right across the main door, in huge red letters, were the words
"Messrs. Pickford's Storage and Collection Depot" and underneath in smaller letters: "Flyboats depart for Liverpool via
Manchester every Tuesday and Thursday at 12 noon."

All three of them looked at this notice in some consternation,
thinking the same thought: Since the trunk containing the
stolen valuables had been collected from the mill on Monday, it
must have already left by the Tuesday-morning boat and by this
time it would be well on its way to Manchester.

"We should have thought of that before," wailed Laura. "We'll
never get our jewelry and silver back now!"

"I shouldn't be too sure about that, miss," said Wally reassur-
ingly. "Canals is funny things—they're sure but slow—and we
might 'ave a chance of catchin' that there flyboat up long before
it gets to Manchester. But right now we'd best concentrate on
catchin' up with that lovesick 'ound of mine—otherwise me
grandsons will be dachshunds!"

They went through the door into the great warehouse.
Everywhere it was stacked with boxes, trunks, and parcels of all
shapes and sizes. At the far end, the great sliding doors were

open, giving directly onto the canal, where the barges and flyboats drew up for loading. Mullinger followed his lady love through these doors and down a flight of stone steps onto a narrow wooden catwalk, which ran right along the backs of all the warehouses. Dodging behind stacks of parcels to avoid the notice of the warehousemen, Wally and the children crept down the steps and along the catwalk just in time to see the dachshund scramble aboard a barge that was moored alongside the next warehouse. Mullinger made no attempt to follow her, but instead waited for the three friends and greeted them with a broad grin and a tailful of wags.

"Well, I'll be blowed," said Wally. " 'E ain't in love after all! 'E never grins when 'e's in love—allus 'as a kind o' pained look, like indigestion. Mullinger, old friend, I apologize. I thought you was in the grip of another foolish passion."

Mullinger's grin broadened and became rather disdainful, as if to say, "Me in love? What a ridiculous idea!"

"But if you ain't in love," Wally went on, "what *are* you up to? There's somethin' fishy about this barge, or you wouldn't 'ave brought us 'ere."

At this moment the barge master appeared from the cabin. He was a short square man with close-cropped ginger hair and cauliflower ears. He was stripped to the waist, and on his chest (as well as coal dust, oil smears, sweat, and a mat of red hair) was a tattoo of a large lady, a heart with an arrow through it, and the words "I Love Mabel." He had a stubby pipe between his teeth, and the tobacco had turned his walrus mustache a bright yellow color, like Leicestershire cheese. He gave the three friends a hostile stare and said:

"I don't take kindly to snoops."

To Laura and Raymond's surprise, Wally replied:

"As a matter of fact, sir, we were wonderin' whether you take passengers on your boat."

"I might, an' I might not," said the barge master. "It depends on the passengers—an' on 'ow much they'd pay."

"Money is no object," said Wally grandly, "but speed is important. We—er—missed the Pickford's flyboat, you see."

"Pickford's'll take a day and 'alf—wot with the load it's carryin'—an' stoppin' to pick stuff up an' put stuff down. I'll 'ave you there in one day—if you make it worth my while."

Wally held up half a sovereign. The barge master turned to go back into his cabin.

Wally held up two half-sovereigns.

"We'll be off at eight in t' mornin'," said the barge master.

7

TROUBLED WATERS

*in which Laura and Raymond travel by barge through
a terrifying tunnel, outtrick a trickster, find a new
friend but lose an old one.*

Raymond asked his mother if she would tidy his bed and give
him his night injection earlier than usual that evening.

"It's going to be a busy day tomorrow," he explained. "We've
got a long journey, and we have to make an early start."

"And where are you off to this time—Timbuktu?" Mrs. Price,
who was busy popping things into a plastic bag to take to the
launderette, smiled.

"No, Manchester—but the day after we'll probably be going to
Liverpool."

Mrs. Price looked at him sadly. Nowadays he seemed to live
almost entirely in his make-believe world. It seemed more and
more difficult to keep the fever down. His sheets and pajamas
now had to be changed twice a day. The laundry bag was bulging
with them.

"Well," she said, "I'll settle you down a *little* earlier if you
like—but not *too* early. For one thing, you know you won't sleep
so well if you have your injection too soon. And for another, the
doctor's going to look in—and"—she hesitated a bit here—"Mr.
Rogers said he would call to have a look at you."

Raymond made a wry face. Mr. Rogers was the vicar of the
local church—the one that had just been demolished. Raymond
had hoped that, when the church disappeared, the vicar would
too, since Mr. Rogers always made him feel uncomfortable. He
wasn't actually unpleasant or unkind; in fact he was a gentle

elderly man who always brought Raymond a bunch of flowers and a box of sweets (though he was forbidden to eat sweets and he didn't like having flowers by his bedside). The main trouble was that Mr. Rogers didn't seem to know what to talk about, so Raymond felt sorry for him and made big efforts to keep the conversation going, which left him feeling tired out at the end of it. When Mr. Rogers *did* say something, it was usually something about religion, which Raymond didn't understand too well. He was supposed to be preparing him for his First Communion and had said that very soon he would "administer the Sacrament." This scared Raymond rather: it sounded like another kind of injection. . . .

As he lay there thinking gloomily of injections, Dr. Reynolds entered the room. He always came in without knocking, which was something Raymond didn't like about *him*.

"Well, now," he said breezily, as he felt Raymond's pulse and listened to his back and chest with his stethoscope, "how are we today? Not too many hair-raising adventures recently, I hope?"

Raymond didn't answer. The doctor went over to Mrs. Price and began to talk to her in a low voice, which Raymond could hear perfectly well. It was funny how adults always thought you couldn't hear what they were saying when they didn't want you to.

"The fever may break within the next forty-eight hours," the doctor said, "but if it doesn't, this may be the terminal illness. I'll arrange for a nurse to come in. If there's any sign of rapid deterioration, he'll have to be hospitalized at once."

The only bit that Raymond really understood was the word "hospitalized," but it didn't worry him too much since he felt quite confident that Wally would find some way of coping with that. He was looking forward to the barge trip very much, even though he knew it was going to be dangerous and difficult, and he was quite sure that Wally wouldn't let him miss it.

So he lay back on his pillow and didn't even notice when the doctor left and his mother slipped out to the launderette. He dozed a bit, perhaps for ten or fifteen minutes, and then was suddenly roused by a tap on the door. His heart sank. This must be Mr. Rogers. For a moment he thought of pretending to be asleep, so that the vicar would go away. But this would be acting a lie, so instead he called out, "Come in," in a very quiet voice, hoping that Mr. Rogers, who was in fact rather deaf, wouldn't hear it. But the door opened, and Raymond saw the familiar dark suit and clergyman's collar. Then, to his surprise, he realized that the face above the collar was not Mr. Rogers' face at all—it was the face of a much younger man with humorous gray eyes, a friendly smile, and dark bushy sideburns that looked very modern and very old-fashioned at the same time.

"Hello," said the young clergyman, "may I come in? My name's Ben Oddy. I'm the curate. Mr. Rogers isn't feeling too well tonight so he sent me around instead."

Raymond felt very relieved. "Mummy's out at the moment," he said. "She's just gone to the launderette, but she'll be back soon, and then she'll make you a cup of tea."

"Perhaps I could make the tea," said the curate. "Then there'll be a cup ready for her when she gets back."

He bustled around for a moment filling the kettle and setting the teacups out on a tray. Then he came and sat down on the edge of the bed. He glanced around the flat.

"I hear you'll be on the move soon," he said in his quiet, lazy-sounding voice.

"Yes," said Raymond, "I'm going to Manchester tomorrow."

"Great," said the curate. "Bus, train, or barge?"

Raymond shot Mr. Oddy a quick glance to see if he was pulling his leg. But the twinkle in the curate's gray eyes was a kindly and interested one—a *serious* twinkle, Raymond decided—so he said:

"Barge for the first part of the journey. Then I'm not sure. It's up to Wally really. He's sort of . . . in charge."

"You don't mean Walter Wilberforce Tulliver, by any chance, do you?"

"Yes," said Raymond, surprised. "Do you know him?"

"Everybody knows him—or at least, he knows everybody. It's ages since I saw him, though—not since I was a kid myself really. But his name keeps cropping up, and I meet people—like you for instance—who've seen him around recently. So I sort of keep in touch that way."

"Do you know Mullinger to?"

"That crazy mixed-up dog," Mr. Oddy laughed. "I know him only too well! Once he gets your scent, he never lets you alone."

They were both silent for a moment as Mr. Oddy chuckled to himself at the thought of Mullinger. Raymond wondered whether to ask him about Laura, but decided not to. Instead, he asked him a different question altogether.

"What's a terminal illness, Mr. Oddy?"

"You don't *have* to call me Mr. Oddy, you know. Most people call me Ben. Well, you're an expert on railways, so you know what a terminal station is."

"It's the last station—the end of the railway, really."

"Well, a terminal illness is the end of an illness."

"Does that mean I shan't be ill anymore?"

"That's exactly what it does mean. Oh, my gosh, the kettle's boiling over!"

He brewed the tea and had just poured himself a cup when Mrs. Price arrived, so he poured one out for her and stayed on for a little longer to chat. Then he got up to go, but before he left he said:

"Oh, I nearly forgot, I've brought you a record. Your mum tells me you like music."

He took a large package from the inside flap of his threadbare duffel coat and tossed it onto the bed. Raymond opened it and looked at the label. His eyes lighted up.

"It's an LP," he cried.

"Yes," said Ben. "It's not a pop record, but I think you may enjoy it," and as he disappeared around the door he called back, "And give my love to Wally."

Mrs. Price left at half past seven next morning. The nurse was due to come in at eight fifteen, but Wally was sure to be there before then.

Raymond suddenly remembered the record Ben had left. He

looked around for it and found that his mother had left it on his bedside table together with the little portable record player that the children from school had sent him last Christmas. He'd collected quite a lot of records since then—all singles, though, so he mustn't forget to switch over to speed 33 before playing this new one. The record had a funny title, Haydn's "Concerto for Trumpet and Orchestra in E Flat." Haydn must be the name of the composer—it couldn't be the name of a group because Ben had said that it wasn't a pop record. Still, it was a trumpet record, and by now the trumpet had become Raymond's favorite instrument. Carefully he fitted the record onto the automatic position and waited for it to click down onto the turntable and for the arm to move across.

At first he was a little disappointed. The orchestra was quite pleasant, but it was mainly violins, which he always thought were rather squeaky instruments, and there didn't seem to be any definite tune. But then, suddenly and unexpectedly but yet (Raymond thought) just at the right moment, the trumpet came through on its own, playing a clear, confident, bold tune which, he could now see, had been present in the opening part played by the violins all the time. The tune was rich and thrilling, and the trumpeter seemed to be enjoying himself as he skated up and down the scales, scattering his silver notes in all directions. But now things became even more exciting, because the rest of the orchestra came back in, and a kind of duel developed between the trumpeter and all the other instruments, each trying to seize and hold on to the tune in turn and to do more daring and difficult things with it. It was more than a duel—it was a battle in which one man seemed to be taking on a whole army single-handed. It reminded him of the picture he had seen in Mrs. Hamilton's room, of Roland blowing his ivory horn, challenging on his own the whole of the Saracen army.

And now a really extraordinary thing happened. The trumpeter, by sheer skill and courage and persistence, forced all the rest of the orchestra into silence, and for several seconds, or minutes—it seemed to Raymond almost like an eternity—he did exactly as he pleased, swooping and darting and curving and soaring and pirouetting in a marvelous one-man display of trumpet technique, climbing daringly up to heights that made Raymond hold his breath for fear the note would crack or waver and then suddenly plunging down to depths that Raymond had imagined only the tuba or the trombone could reach. And then, just at the moment when the trumpeter's conquest was complete, he brought the tune back to the orchestra, and they all joined in joyfully together, so that what had seemed like a victory for one instrument alone became in the end a victory for them all.

As the record clicked off and Raymond lay back on his pillow (for he had been sitting bolt upright in sheer astonishment), he felt that he understood what that music had been saying to him. But he couldn't put it into words, and he didn't even try to. He just felt filled with peace—the kind of peace that comes just at the moment of achieving something very difficult or very dangerous. He was so happy just to lie there with this feeling that he didn't notice for ages that Wally had entered the room and had perched himself on the end of the bed, with Mullinger at his feet. And it was not until Wally finally spoke that Raymond realized that he had been in the room all the time, even while the record was playing.

"Marvelous things, them old trumpet concertos," said Wally. "Of course, they were written for *real* trumpets—not these newfangled modern things with valves."

"Were the old-fashioned trumpets very different?" asked Raymond in surprise.

"You bet your life they were," said Wally. "For one thing, they could reach a much 'igher pitch than the modern ones."

"But the trumpeter on the record reached all the high notes," said Raymond, puzzled, "and *he* must have been playing a modern instrument."

"Ah," said Wally, with a confidential wink, "that's where you're wrong. There are just a few of the old 'uns still kicking around. In fact, this 'ere instrument of mine . . . "

He put it to his lips and played a few notes. Raymond recognized them immediately as the topmost notes of the solo he had just heard.

"You sound exactly like the record," he cried delightedly, but before he could ask Wally to play any more, he heard footsteps on the pavement outside and saw, to his horror, the blue-uniformed figure of the nurse coming down the basement steps.

"Quick," said Wally, dragging aside the kitchen screen. "We'd best dodge in 'ere. Business before pleasure, I always say. There'll be plenty of time for music when we get back!"

Mrs. Porson's kitchen seemed full of people. Laura was there, busily supervising Clara and Hannah, who were buttering bread and making egg-and-chutney sandwiches. Laura had also brought Philomena, Sadie, and Mary Ellen down to help in the kitchen, and they were hard at work slicing up a game pie, a cold saddle of mutton, and a gooseberry-and-apple tart, wrapping the separate portions neatly in greaseproof paper and packing them into two small baskets (the kind with shoulder straps that anglers often seem to carry around). Mrs. Porson meanwhile was stuffing eggs with prawns and keeping an eye on some mincemeat pies and Cornish pasties, which were nearly ready in the large oven. P. C. Crumble was sitting at a corner table, picking rather gloomily at a pickled herring and a piece of dry toast.

"Good morning, ladies," said Wally cheerfully, "and good morning to you too, Constable. I'm glad to see that once again we have the protection of the strong arm of the law."

"Strong arm of the law indeed!" sniffed Mrs. Porson. "If 'e'd bin a bit stronger in the 'ead instead o' th'arm, 'e wouldn't 'ave bin fooled by that smart London lawyer like 'e was yesterday."

She gave the constable a disdainful look. He pretended to be concentrating on his herring, which was indeed so skinny and so full of bones that it was taking him all his time to pick the flesh off it. Wally cleared his throat to speak, but Mrs. Porson went on:

"It's more brains and less brawn that some folk need! Now, take yerself, Mr. Wally. You're not wot I'd call a big man, though"—eyeing him appreciatively with a roguish blush—"you've an 'andsome figure, but the best of it is, you've got yer 'ead screwed on right an' you don't make a fool of yerself in public, like some folk I could mention."

The slightly hunted look came back to Wally's eye. Mrs. Porson was advancing on him with a couple of freshly baked Cornish pasties and a mug of porter. It was Philomena who unexpectedly came to the rescue. She sidled over to the constable with a slice of game pie and said:

"Don't you be mindin' what she says, Constable. You're a darlin' man and a handsome one too, and how can you be expected to outwit the London lawyers, and you without ever a square meal to fill your belly at all?"

"Quite right, miss," said Wally eagerly, "quite right. Those are exactly my sentiments. The constable needs feedin', that's all. Might I suggest, ma'am, that we offer 'im one of these delicious Cornish pasties. . . . "

"And a couple of stuffed eggs for good measure," chimed in Philomena, seating herself on the constable's knee and slipping her arm around his neck.

For Mrs. Porson this was the last straw. She dropped the plate of Cornish pasties (they were swiftly demolished by Mullinger) and slammed the pint of porter down on the table. Purple with rage, she hurled a stuffed egg at Wally (which missed) and another one at Philomena and the constable (which landed with a soft *phut* on the constable's pink cheek). Then she sat down at the table, put her head between her arms, and unexpectedly burst into floods of tears. Laura and the maids flocked around to render assistance, while Raymond, Wally, and the constable hung back in alarm.

"It's me 'eart," wailed Mrs. Porson between her sobs. "It's me poor womanly 'eart wot's torn in two. Wally . . . Cedric . . . I know you both love me"—here Wally and Cedric looked at each other in alarm—"but the trouble is I can't for the life o' me make up my mind which one of you to take! That's the reason for me tantrums and me tempers—it's me poor 'eart wot's torn in two!"

Once again she dissolved into incoherent sobs. Laura produced a bottle of smelling salts and said:

"Dear Cook, do not distress yourself. We have to set off on our journey now, and no doubt the constable has to return to duty too. We shall be away for a while, so perhaps during that time matters will become clearer to you. Keep calm, and look after the house during our absence, and you will find that everything will turn out for the best in the end."

Laura's kind words and the soothing effects of the smelling salts soon restored the cook to herself. Still sniffing a little, and occasionally drawing a huge shuddering sigh, she bustled about the kitchen seeing to the final packing of the baskets. Meanwhile Wally was deep in consultation with Laura and Raymond.

"All we need to take," he said, "is enough grub to last us to Manchester and back. If we can catch up with that trunk, then we're sure to catch up with Smarmling, for 'e'll be waitin' there to collect it, sure as eggs. Once we've got that settled, we can think about settlin' more important matters in Liverpool."

"But," said Raymond hesitantly, "wouldn't it be better for someone to stay behind to keep an eye on that train—just in case Laura's father can be rescued before they get him away in the caboose?"

"I've made . . . er . . . certain arrangements as regards that train," said Wally, "and Mullinger 'ere is stayin' be'ind to take care of 'em. Right, Mullinger?"

Mullinger looked up from under the constable's chair, where he was sniffing around for any more stuffed eggs that might have been used as missiles. He wagged his tail briefly to indicate that he'd understood his instructions.

"And don't forget to keep in touch with P. C. Crumble," added Wally. "A man like 'im, with a strong arm and . . . er . . . a cool 'ead can be very useful to a dog in an emergency."

Mullinger gave another wag, accompanied by a grin. P. C.

Crumble strapped on his helmet and braced his shoulders with a businesslike air.

A few moments later, after hurried farewells, the kitchen was empty except for Mrs. Porson and the kitchen maids, who addressed themselves in silence to the task of cleaning up the floor and preparing the barrels of soup for the hungry workfolk.

The barge was moored in the same place when Wally and the children arrived somewhat breathlessly on the catwalk behind the warehouses. It was a long, narrow boat, dark brown in color except for the fancy paintwork on the sloping gunwales and the sides of the cabin. The cabin itself was right up in front of the barge, and had a flat top and a metal chimney. The prow, which was carved into the shape of a dragon's head, jutted out just in front of the main cabin door. On the side panel of the cabin was painted the boat's registration number, its tonnage, and the name of the company that owned it—"The Blackstone and Stourport Canal Co. Ltd." Just below this, on the gunwale, was the name of the boat—the *Lady Mabel.*

The barge master was on the towpath on the opposite side of the canal, fixing the towrope to the harness of a huge white horse with flowing white mane and fetlocks. In spite of his size, the horse looked bony and underfed. He turned his mournful eyes across to where they stood, and Raymond felt sorry for the poor beast, especially when he saw how roughly the barge master was tugging at his bit and harness in order to get the towrope adjusted properly.

The bargeman showed no sign of recognition. He gave a last vicious tug at the harness straps, walked back along the towpath, and crossed back over a little footbridge to the warehouse side. Even when he got to the barge, he simply climbed on board without greeting his passengers and disappeared into the cabin. At length he emerged and gave them a surly glare.

"Get aboard then," he said, "you're wastin' good time." But as they began to clamber over the gunwale, he added, "I can't tek all three—one of you will 'ave to lead the 'oss."

"Oh, please, may I?" cried Laura and Raymond both at once, but Wally said:

"Better if you two go aboard for a start off. Then when we get clear into the country, we'll take turns."

This was agreed, so the children climbed aboard while Wally cast off the mooring rope and trotted over the footbridge to catch up with the horse, who had already started to amble forward in response to a whistle from the barge master. As the barge glided out into the middle of the canal, the children settled themselves on the flat roof of the cabin while the barge master clambered back across the piles of limestone chippings and granite blocks, which were his cargo, and took the tiller in the stern of the boat.

It was all strange and rather frightening to Raymond at first, because he had never been on a boat before, except once on a children's boating pond when he was very tiny. Laura also found it rather scary because, although she had once been on a holiday to France with her father, she had been seasick on the Channel crossing and was wondering whether the slight swaying of the barge would make her seasick again. So they sat very close together, holding hands tightly and afraid to move in case they slipped off the cabin roof into the gloomy water.

But after a while, as they got used to the movement of the boat, they began to enjoy it and take an interest in the sights and sounds of the canal bank. Sometimes they met other barges coming the opposite way, and then, since the towpath ran along only one side of the canal, one horse had to stand still and let its rope go slack while the other horse plodded past and its rope was handed over the top of the waiting barge. Sometimes, too, they came to small bridges where the towpath ended, and then the horse had to be unhitched and led around to the other side of the bridge while the bargeman propelled the boat through the tunnel like a punt, by means of a large pole. Each time this happened, the barge master cursed and swore, and ordered the children to help him keep the boat moving by lying flat on the cabin roof and heaving with their legs against the sides of the tunnel. He was too mean to employ the poor ragged men or boys who usually waited at the bridges hoping to earn a copper or two by legging the barges through the tunnels. Raymond noticed, though, that Wally always stopped to have a word with these "leggers" as he led the horse around the bridge, and that they always looked very pleased with themselves as the barge finally drew away.

Soon they had left the gloomy mills and warehouses of the town behind them, and were out in the open country. The fields were thick with lush high grass, where cattle were peacefully grazing. In places dense trees overhung the canal, and Raymond and Laura enjoyed themselves tearing off branches and trailing them in the water. As the sun climbed higher in the sky, they lay back on the warm cabin roof, dozing and listening to the ripple and gurgle of the water on the sides of the barge, forgetful of everything except the happiness of being together.

Suddenly they became aware that the rippling had stopped and the barge had come to a standstill. Sitting up, they saw that they had come to a tollgate and that the keeper was coming toward the barge to check the cargo and collect the toll. Raymond knew that every barge had to pay a toll, and that the amount depended on the kind of cargo that was being carried. Much more had to be paid on valuable cargoes like merchandise than on cheap cargoes like sand or building materials. As the tollgate keeper stepped on board carrying his collecting bag and receipt book, Raymond thought he noticed a sly grin pass between him and the barge master. Something prompted him to whisper to Laura, "Lie down again and pretend to be dozing," but instead of lying on their backs they now lay on their sides with their heads on their arms, keeping their eyes and ears open for what was going on at the stern of the boat.

"Mornin', Mr. Kieran," said the keeper.

"Mornin', Mr. Keeper," said the barge master.

"Granite and limestone as usual?" said the keeper.

"Granite and limestone it is," said the barge master.

"Mind if I inspect it?" said the keeper.

"Inspect wot you like," said the barge master.

The keeper poked and prodded with his foot among the limestone chippings and granite blocks. After a few moments, he bent down and began burrowing among the chippings with his hands. Underneath, he unearthed a trunk, locked with two padlocks and stuck over with labels.

"Would you mind openin' this trunk?" he said.

"I ain't got no key," said the barge master.

"Them labels 'ave a Pickford's stamp on 'em," said the keeper.

"That's true," said the barge master.

"I don't suppose, now, that it contains granite and limestone?" said the keeper.

"I don't suppose it does," said the barge master.

"Perhaps I ought to report you to the company," said the keeper.

"But I don't think you will," said the bargee. He produced four half-crowns from his pocket and slipped them into the keeper's hand.

"You're right," said the keeper, pocketing the money and covering up the box with the chippings. "In fact, I 'aven't even noticed that chest. But I'll trouble you to pay toll on twenty tons o' limestone and granite."

"It's a pleasure," said the bargee, handing over more money, which this time went into the collecting-bag, and receiving an official receipt in return.

"Mornin', Mr. Kieran," said the keeper.

"Mornin', Mr. Keeper," said the barge master.

As the tollgates swung open and the barge glided through, Laura and Raymond stared at each other in amazement.

"Do you think . . . ?" whispered Raymond.

"Yes," said Laura, "I'm certain. That is Miss Peach's traveling chest, and our valuables are in it. The barge master must have stolen it from Pickford's warehouse, and he's bribed the tollgate man to let it through."

"What shall we do?" said Raymond.

"It'll be our turn to lead the horse soon," said Laura, "so when we change over, we'll ask Wally. He's sure to think of a plan."

Two miles beyond the tollgate there was a pub called The Jolly Bargeman. Here the barge master brought the boat into the bank and called out to Wally to unhitch the towrope. Then he tethered the horse to a tree and put on its nose bag—though with hardly any oats in it.

"We stop 'ere to eat," he said, and disappeared into the pub. But Wally and the children, who were not standing on the bank by the horse, noticed that he took up his position by the pub door where he could keep an eye on his barge.

The children were bursting to tell Wally their news, but he stopped them almost before they had begun and said:

"Pleasure before business, that's my motto. I'd like to examine the contents of them baskets, afore we start discussin' the contents of that trunk."

He untethered the horse and led him down into a grassy hollow where he could graze on fresh grass and drink from a little brook. Laura set out the picnic on the spotless white tablecoth that Mrs. Porson had provided, while Wally paddled in the brook to cool his hot feet and Raymond (who had just joined the Cubs before he became ill) built a little camp fire even though they had no matches to light it with and no kettle to boil water in. Then, as they started in on the Cornish pasties and stuffed eggs, Wally listened carefully to the children's tale, nodding from time to time as if he was not a bit surprised at what they told him. At the end of it, he was silent for a while, and then he said unexpectedly:

"What's in the second basket?"

"Apples, mostly," said Laura, feeling rather disappointed because Wally seemed more interested in the food than in their story.

"Good," said Wally, "let's call Snowdrift in to 'elp us eat them."

He made a clucking noise with his tongue, and the great white horse came ambling over to where they sat, his silky hair lifting and rippling in the light breeze. Raymond was rather scared at first of offering him an apple—his lips and teeth seemed so enormous when you got close to them—but Laura, who had a pony of her own, showed him how to hold the apple on the palm of his hand so that Snowdrift could scoop it up without biting his fingers. After one or two tries, Raymond began to enjoy feeling the warm velvety muzzle pressing into his hand so gently, and watching the huge teeth chomping and crunching away at the small sweet apples they offered him. Then, to Raymond's delight, Wally suggested a ride around the field, so, using an old tree trunk as a mounting block, all three of them clambered up (Raymond at the front holding tight to the harness, Laura in the middle, and Wally at the back) and Snowdrift trotted around and around, snorting with pleasure as Raymond patted his neck and fondled his ears.

When at last they dismounted, they gave Snowdrift the rest of the apples and finished off the gooseberry pie themselves.

"Right now," said Wally, "we've got four full bellies and two empty baskets, so we're in a position to make our plans. Now listen carefully. About a mile farther on the canal goes underground—they've tunneled right through Alum Scar, which is the last of the big 'ills around these parts. It's a long tunnel, and the bargeman'll 'ave to employ leggers to shove the boat through while 'e attends to the tiller, 'cause it's tricky navigatin' too. Now if Laura takes Snowdrift from 'ere on, she can lead 'im over the 'ill when we get to Alum Tunnel, while Raymond and I stay on board to 'elp leg the boat through. But we won't be doin' any leggin' because we'll be busy with another little job!"

He gave them a wink, but they both looked at him blankly.

"What will we be doing?" asked Raymond.

"We'll be emptyin' that trunk and packin' the stuff in these baskets."

"But the trunk is padlocked," said Laura, "doubly padlocked!"

Wally grinned. "You're forgettin', miss, that you're talkin' to a professional escape artist. Padlocks is no problem. The great 'Oudini himself taught me a thing or two about padlocks."

"Houdini?" said Laura, puzzled.

"Sorry, miss, I was forgettin' 'e lived after your time. You could put 'Oudini in a straitjacket, fasten 'im round with chains, lock 'im in a tea chest, an' chuck 'im in the Thames—but 'e'd wriggle out o' the lot an' bob up large as life! Padlocks was the least of 'is problems—'e could open 'em with 'is toes!"

"But," said Raymond, still looking doubtful, "even if you *can* open the trunk, the barge master will see us. He'll be sitting at the tiller, just a few feet away."

Wally grinned again. "Ain't you forgettin' that this is a long tunnel—and a *dark* 'un?"

"But it won't be *pitch*-dark," objected Raymond. "Even long train tunnels let *some* light through, as your eyes get accustomed to it."

"Ah," said Wally, "but this ain't a train tunnel—it's a canal tunnel, and there's a difference. Train tunnels are built in a straight line, so the light filters through from one end to the other. But water 'as to follow the curve of the earth, so canal tunnels are curved—and they're pitch-black in the middle 'cause light can't bend round corners!"

Raymond nodded. Mr. Jeffars had once shown them an experiment at school to prove that light beams move in straight lines. But as they walked slowly back to the barge with the empty baskets slung over their shoulders, his heart was full of fear at the thought of entering that black hole and stealing the treasure from under the very nose of the brutal bargeman.

When they got back to the towpath, the barge master was just coming out of the pub. His face was flushed, and he was walking rather unsteadily. As he clambered aboard the barge, he emitted a loud hiccup. Wally winked at Raymond and whispered:

"He's 'alf drunk—so he won't notice so much."

But when Raymond caught sight of the evil cunning glint in Kieran's eye, he didn't feel very comforted by Wally's reassuring words. Nor did he feel any happier when, as the boat glided along, the barge master began swaying from side to side and singing in a drunken, throaty voice:

"I was born about ten thousand years ago
And there's nothin' in this world that I don't know.
I saw Peter, Paul, and Moses playin' ring-a-ring-a-roses
And I'll kill the bloke wot says it isn't so.

"I saw Satan when 'e looked the garden o'er,
I saw Eve an' Adam driven from the door,
From behind the bushes peepin' seen the apple they was eatin'
And I'll swear that I'm the bloke wot ate the core. . . "

So they drifted on, nearer and nearer to the great craggy mass
of Alum Scar, until Raymond could distinctly see the gaping
black mouth of the tunnel and the usual little crowd of leggers
waiting hopefully on the towpath. Kieran brought the boat to
the tunnel opening, unhitched Snowdrift, and curtly ordered
Laura to lead him over the bridle path that wound its way
around the side of the hill. Then he picked out four tattered
urchins from among the leggers and said:
     " 'Ow much?"
     "Penny each," said the first.
     Kieran just scowled.
     "It's an 'eavy boat," said the second.
     Another scowl.
     "We'll do it for an 'a-penny," said the third.
     "Penny between us then," said the fourth.
     The barge master nodded, and the leggers came abroad, each
carrying a plank to lie across the boat so as to get a better push
against the tunnel walls. Wally and Raymond also lay down on
top of the cargo, and slowly, powered by six sets of straining legs,
the barge entered the tunnel.
     At first Raymond could make things out quite easily in the
gloom. He could see the great stone blocks of the tunnel wall,
upon which, here and there, people had scribbled names or
initials with chalk or limestone. He could see too the greenish-
black slime on the lower parts of the walls, rising a foot or two
above the surface of the water. He could even, dimly, make out

the forms and faces of his companions—Wally pedaling away at the walls with his sturdy little legs, and the four small boys in front of him, pinched and starved-looking, with legs almost as thin as the tails of the water rats which from time to time plopped into the canal from some slimy ledge or cranny. Now and again the wall was built back into a little alcove, and as Raymond peered into these dank and dismal caves, his nostrils caught the stench of the rotting garbage that had been washed onto their stagnant surfaces, and he shivered to think that he might be passing within a few feet of some ghastly decomposing corpse. But quite soon, as Wally had predicted, the last feebly filtering rays of light were swallowed up in a blackness so intense and impenetrable that Raymond could not even see his own hands clasping an iron ring on the gunwale an inch or two before his eyes.

"Now's our chance!" whispered Wally, easing himself over from the gunwale to the center of the boat, but just as Raymond was about to follow suit, he was horrified to see the whole of the stern part of the boat suddenly illuminated with a dazzling light. The bargee had lighted an oil lamp!

"Wot the 'ell are you up to?" he snapped viciously as he spotted Wally crawling amidships on all fours.

Wally was taken aback but quickly recovered his presence of mind. "I was wonderin'," he said, unbuttoning his knapsack, "if you'd care to join me in a tot or two o' rum, to warm us up, like, in this chilly old tunnel?"

He produced a small flask labeled "Lamb's Old English Navy Rum" and held it up for Kieran's inspection. The barge master's little pig eyes glittered with greed.

"You 'ave the first swig," said Wally, "while I 'old the lamp for you."

He crawled to the stern seat, perched himself on it next to the bargeman and exchanged the rum bottle for the lamp. The bargeman took a huge gulp, smacked his lips in appreciation, and passed the bottle back to Wally. Wally took a sip, and the lamp and bottle changed hands again. Three times this happened, and then, to Raymond's amazement, Wally stuck up a song in a drunken voice:

> "Fifteen men on a dead man's chest
> Yo ho ho and a bottle of rum."

The barge master joined in the chorus with rough bass grunts. So they sat there, swaying and singing, passing and repassing the bottle and the lamp, until with a final greedy gulp, Kieran drained the last dregs of the rum. Wally now stood up, still clutching the lamp, and began to do a lurching, staggering dance on the uneven surface of the granite blocks, singing as he did so:

> "What shall we do with a drunken sailor?
> What shall we do with a drunken sailor?
> What shall we ... "

But before he got any further he fell flat on his face among the limestone chippings. The lamp shot from his hand, flew over the gunwale, and disappeared with a fizz into the dark, slimy water.

The barge master's hoarse guffaws turned to a yell of rage. Out of the blackness which now muffled them again like a thick blanket, his voice went on screaming and cursing, but Wally took no notice of it. Instead, he scrambled over to Raymond and whispered urgently:

" 'Elp me get at that trunk. We've only five minutes to find it, pick the locks, and empty it!"

Raymond had remembered the exact spot where the trunk lay under the limestone, but in the pitch-darkness it was no easy task to get his bearings. Fortunately the barge master was still cursing, and Wally enraged him still more by beginning to sing again in a tipsy voice, so the noise of Raymond's scrapings and scrabblings among the boulders and chippings could not easily be heard. At last he felt the smooth wood of the box lid, and he groped for Wally's hands to place them on the padlocks.

Then began for Raymond an agony of waiting as the seconds

ticked relentlessly by, eating up a minute, then two minutes, then two and a half minutes of their precious time—and still Wally had not released even the first of the two padlocks. It was only when Raymond was almost certain that the darkness was thinning out a little that a nudge from Wally told him that the locks had been picked and that it was time to put the jewels and silver in the baskets.

This *could* have been done in just a few seconds by tipping the contents out bodily from one container to another, but instead it had to be done slowly and warily, piece by piece and trinket by trinket, to avoid the slightest clink or clatter. To make things worse, the bargeman had stopped cursing and was now sitting in morose silence a few feet away, and Raymond could almost *feel* those little sharp eyes piercing the darkness. Oh, how precious that darkness now seemed to him, though it had seemed so dreadful when he first entered the tunnel! He could almost wish to stay in the darkness for ever rather than emerge into the sunlight again without the treasure he had set his heart on recovering, for Laura and her father's sake.

Then suddenly he had an idea. If Wally played his trumpet, it would cover up a lot of the noise, and he could work faster. But before he even mentioned it, Wally seemed to have read his thoughts. He raised his trumpet and began to play a slow clear tune which echoed strangely through the tunnel, keeping rhythm with the movements of the thin straining legs of the four little boys who were pushing the heavy barge slowly but surely toward the light:

> Swing low, sweet chariot,
> Coming for to carry me home,
> Swing low, sweet chariot,
> Coming for to carry me home. . . .
>
> I looked over Jordan and what did I see
> Coming for to carry me home?
> A band of angels coming after me,
> Coming for to carry me home. . . .

The barge master was so taken aback by this sudden flood of sound—or even perhaps touched deep down inside himself by its haunting beauty—that he sat as if mesmerized, so that even though the tunnel mouth was now coming into sight he didn't seem to notice Raymond's last frantic efforts to fasten the stuffed baskets and replace the empty box under the loose chippings. When finally the music died away and he did come to his senses, Raymond and Wally were both back in their places legging away at the walls, and there was nothing, except perhaps a rather *too* innocent expression on Wally's face, to show Kieran that he had been robbed of his treasure.

Laura was waiting at the other end of the tunnel. She had ridden Snowdrift around the bridle path, and by this time they had become so fond of each other that she was rather reluctant to go back into the barge. So she and Raymond agreed that they would both lead him for the next stage of the journey, and this gave Raymond a chance to tell her all about their adventures in the tunnel. It also gave Wally a chance to transfer his basket to Laura, but the baskets were now so heavy that the children strapped them together and hung them like panniers over Snowdrift's broad back.

So they clip-clopped forward, sometimes riding and sometimes walking, making good time until at last they came in sight of the famous five-rise locks at Ringley. A boat had already entered the first of the five locks when they arrived there, so they had to wait until it had gone through before the *Lady Mabel* could take her turn. The children were fascinated to watch the locks in action, and soon they were running up and down the terraced banks and across the black-and-white wooden bridges, helping the lock keeper's boy to open and shut the sluices by twisting the iron handles shaped like cow horns, or to push open the heavy lock gates each time the sluices had brought the water levels equal. Each lock was like a deep box-shaped well, and when the sluices were opened, the water jetted through the vents like a cataract into the lock below, and the boat above sank lower and lower like a forlorn whale trapped in a gigantic leaking fish tank.

By the time it was the *Lady Mabel*'s turn to enter the top lock the children thoroughly understood what had to be done. They unhitched Snowdrift and led him down to the very bottom of the staircase of locks, where they tethered him on the towpath by a little plot of juicy grass. Then they ran back up to the top lock, into which the *Lady Mabel* was just being legged and punted by the combined efforts of Wally and the barge master, and, at a signal from the lock keeper's boy, they opened the first set of sluices and watched the barge slowly sink away into the bottom of the basin while the water in the next basin gradually rose to meet it. So step by step they lowered the boat until it reached the fifth and last lock. At this moment, just as the boat was beginning to descend for the final time, a smart pony and trap came bowling along a little side road that led to the towpath. The children, who were operating the sluice handles, glanced at the trap—and suddenly froze with fear. Sitting in the driver's seat—and now actually getting out and coming toward them—was the ponderous puffed-out figure of Mr. Smarmling!

So amazed were they to see him there that they stood petrified, unable to run or even to think. Then it dawned on them, when they saw the startled expression on his bloated face, that *he* was equally amazed to see *them*, but this realization came too late, for he quickly overcame his surprise and grabbed them, one in each of his pale pudgy hands.

"If you two brats have been interfering again," he growled, "I'll finish you for good this time!" Then he dragged them over to the edge of the lock basin and called down to the barge master:

"Kieran, have you got the stuff through safely?"

"Safe and sound, Mr. Smarmling." He cleared away the rubble and revealed the trunk.

"Check the contents," snapped Smarmling, tossing down a key but still keeping a viciously tight grip on the children.

Kieran caught the key, jerked open the padlocks, and threw open the lid of the trunk. He uttered a snarl of surprise and rage.

Smarmling's face too was contorted with fury, because even though the boat had now sunk far below him he could see from the bargeman's reaction that the trunk was empty. In a paroxysm of anger he shook Laura violently by the hair and aimed a savage kick at Raymond. But that kick was his undoing. His foot slipped on a patch of moss and he staggered wildly, letting go of the children in a desperate effort to recover his balance. For a moment he tottered on the brink of the basin, his arms flailing like a bird's wings. Then with a squeal of panic, he pitched headfirst over into the lock, plummeting down like a sack of flour and landing with a squelchy splash in the murky water far below. There he floundered and puffed, gulping in gallons of filth and slime, until the barge master hooked him by the suspenders and landed him like an oversized seal amid the rubble in the stern.

Meanwhile Wally had been watching these events from the cabin roof, unable to decide exactly what to do for the best. The bargeman now lunged at him furiously and yanked him by the leg into the stern.

"You 'ideous little dwarf," he yelled, "I'll do for you!"—and, to the children's horror, he rammed Wally brutally into the open trunk, snapped the padlocks shut, and heaved it overboard into the water, where it sank at once like a stone. Then he scrambled across the cabin roof and leaped from the boat to the lockgates, which were constructed of thick horizontal beams, forming a kind of ladder right to the top. Fortunately for the children, he was still too drunk to climb very fast on the wet beams at the bottom, so while he was still slithering and sliding about, Laura and Raymond rushed back to the last set of sluice handles and opened them. Immediately Kieran was attacked by powerful jets of water, which brushed him like a fly from his precarious handhold on the beams. Then, without even waiting to see if their trick had been successful, and forgetting all about Wally's plight in their panic, they fled down to the towpath, leaped onto Snowdrift's back, and galloped away across the fields in the direction of home.

8

A RACE BY RAILWAY

in which Wally and the children catch a train, Hiram P. Harper misses a boat, and P. C. Crumble covers himself with clay and glory.

Raymond had had a bad night. The doctor had been called again, and Raymond woke up with confused memories of his mother's frightened face peering down at him while he writhed under the doctor's clumsy and painful jabs. Now in the morning she looked pale and worn out, and her eyes were red and puffy, as if she had been crying. But she put on a brave smile when she saw he was awake and silently watching her.

"Isn't it nice, dear, I've got a day off today. I've got things to pack and lots of arrangements to make because today will be our last full day here. The moving men will be coming first thing in the morning—and only just in time too, because the demolition team is already starting on next door!"

Raymond could hear them banging and thudding around in the hollow empty house, whistling and singing the latest pop songs while they tore out the huge ornamental mantels and marble fireplaces which—so Raymond had heard—they sold for a good price to antique dealers. But their cheerful songs failed to raise his spirits this morning. His body ached all over, and his heart felt heavy. Slowly he searched his mind, trying to find the reason for the unbearable weight of misery that pressed on him. Then he remembered, and his face flushed with shame and grief: he had lost Wally—left him to die of suffocation in that dreadful box in the filthy water of the canal.

As they had ridden home on Snowdrift, Laura had tried to comfort him, pointing out that Wally was certain to escape, just as the great Houdini had escaped from even more desperate situations. But Raymond was not convinced. He hadn't really believed those stories about Houdini even while Wally had been telling them, and now, as he lay in bed feeling sick and depressed, he doubted whether such a person as Houdini had ever existed.

"Mummy?"

"Yes, dear?"

"Have you ever heard of . . . Houdini?"

Mrs. Price pondered for a moment.

"Well, yes, I believe I have. There was something on television about him a while ago, but I was ironing and I didn't take that much notice of it. He was a stage magician, I think—or perhaps it was a stunt man."

"What's a stunt man?"

"They do the dangerous parts in films—like crashing cars or falling from rooftops. They use all sorts of tricks to make it look real."

"Did Houdini use tricks—or did he *really* do the things people say he did?"

"Oh, I expect it was mostly tricks—like all these conjurers and suchlike."

Raymond lay quiet again, thinking this over. At least his mother had *heard* of Houdini, so Wally wasn't just making it all up. But she didn't really believe in his extraordinary powers of escape, so perhaps Wally was exaggerating. Raymond didn't know what to believe. All he knew was that he couldn't bear now to live without Wally and without Laura and without the hope of finding Laura's father. Perhaps this last hope was the most important thing of all to him now. Raymond couldn't remember his own father, and Mrs. Price never mentioned him and didn't even seem to have any photographs of him—so Raymond had sort of adopted Laura's father as his own, and he felt certain that Mr. Hamilton wouldn't mind.

Thinking that Raymond had dozed off again, Mrs. Price slipped out of the flat on the first of her errands. But there was no chance of dozing—the demolition men were making too much racket. They were banging so hard on an adjoining wall that bits of plaster began to crumble and patter to the floor in Raymond's room. And what was the song they were singing as they hammered? It wasn't a pop song—in fact it was a pretty old song—and yet it was familiar somehow. . . . Ah, yes, now he knew what it was—it was one of those old Negro spirituals that Mr. Jeffars used to get them to sing at morning assembly sometimes instead of the usual dull hymns from *The School Hymnal:*

> "Joshua fit the battle of Jericho, Jericho, Jericho,
> Joshua fit the battle of Jericho
> And the walls came a-tumbling down."

That was it. Now it was all coming back to him, the story of how Joshua's warriors marched around the city of Jericho for six days, and then on the seventh day they marched around seven times and the priests blew their rams'-horn trumpets, and the people gave a great shout, and the walls of the city fell flat. But now the hammering next door was getting so loud that Raymond had to sit up and strain his ears to catch the words:

> "You may talk about your King of Gideon
> You may talk about your man of Saul
> But there's none like good old Joshua
> At the battle of Jericho."

On the word "Jericho," which the singers stretched into a long-drawn-out note, Raymond's heart suddenly leaped, for he thought he heard, behind all the banging and crashing, the vibrant note of a trumpet; but he couldn't be sure, because the whole room was echoing with the noise, so much so that the kitchen screen tottered and fell with a crash and a huge hole appeared in the plaster by the side of the sink. Then the rest of the words came through loud and clear, and, though Raymond was scared to find the bed vibrating and the plaster falling like snow on his bedspread, he forgot his fear and joined in the rousing chorus:

> "Many a victory was Gideon's
> Many a victory was Saul's,
> But there's none like good old Joshua
> When he blew down Jericho walls."

As the chorus reached its climax, another huge lump of plaster fell away, and Wally appeared in a gaping hole in the wall, blowing like mad on his trumpet and doing a little busker's dance like the first time Raymond had seen him.

Raymond leaped out of bed and ran straight through the wall and into his arms.

"Just in time for breakfast," said Wally, beaming delightedly and giving Raymond a big hug. "It'll have to be a quick one, though, 'cause somethin' tells me we're goin' to 'ave another busy day. What's on the menu, Mrs. Porson?"

Mrs. Porson patted a wanton ringlet into place and handed him Laura's breakfast list: "THURSDAY: Broiled kippers, baked eggs, veal cake, fresh fruit in season, marmalade, jam, honey, butter, dry toast, rolls, coffee, tea, hot and cold milk."

"I'll just 'ave kippers and 'oney toast, I think, ma'am," said Wally, adding to Raymond by way of explanation, "Fish is good for the brain, and 'oney gives you strength—an' we're goin' to need plenty of both today."

They had just sat down at the table when Laura came in, looking all fresh and pink and excited.

"I've just been to feed Snowdrift," she said, "and to make sure he's comfortable in his new stall. He's had a good grooming, and he looks lovely! I've given instructions for him to be taken out to the paddock later on, and when Papa comes back, we'll find him a nice easy job at the mill."

Wally nodded approvingly. "Somehow I don't think our friend Mr. Kieran will be needin' 'im again. By the time they 'auled 'im out o' that lock 'e didn't want to see another barge or barge 'oss for the rest of 'is life!"

"What happened to Smarmling?" asked Raymond.

"Would you believe it," said Wally, " 'e'd bin tryin' to double-cross Miss Peach all along. That's why 'e'd paid Kieran to steal 'er trunk from Pickford's—so that 'e could ditch 'er and clear off with the loot on 'is own. But she were waitin' for 'im when 'e crawled out o' the lock. Last I saw of 'em she were chasin' 'im along the towpath with 'er umbrella, hurlin' abuse an' Scripture at 'im for all she were worth!"

"Serves 'im right, the old 'ippocrit!" snorted Mrs. Porson, and then she added, with an affectionate and meaning look at Wally, "There'll be a good job as butler goin' 'ere when Mr. 'Amilton gets back. Cook an' butler makes a good married team."

Wally choked on his kipper and rose hastily from the table. "I think I'm a bit on the small side for buttlin', ma'am, and I don't think I could talk posh enough either."

"Talkin' posh hisn't all that 'ard," said Mrs. Porson, making the attempt. "Hit's only a matter of pickin' up a few haitches."

Wally didn't look convinced, but he was saved the trouble of further reply by the sudden entrance of Mullinger, who was dragging Constable Crumble along on the end of his leash. The constable flopped into a chair, unstrapped his helmet, and mopped his perspiring brow.

"That hanimal," he said, "is a menace to the 'ooman race. 'E 'asn't given me a minute's peace since you left yesterday. 'E's bin worritin' for me to foller 'im every bit o' the time, an' draggin' me from one end o't'town to t'other. All 'e does when 'e gets there is 'ave a sniff, an' then 'e drags me all the way back. I were sound asleep in bed this mornin'—after a very 'ectic night with 'im—when 'e comes scratchin' and scrabblin' at me lodgin's until my landlady could stand no more of it. So she lets 'im up into me bedroom, an' wot does 'e do? 'E wakes me up with 'is big wet nose in me ear 'ole, gives me a silly bit o' ribbon, an' pesters me to bring 'im 'ere! An' now 'e wants to be off somewhere else, just like I told you!"

Mullinger indeed was pawing and whining at the door and jerking his head at the others to tell them to follow. But they didn't need much telling because as soon as they saw the crumpled bit of red ribbon that the constable was clutching in his sweaty fingers, they knew that it had come from Mr. Hamilton and that the train must be leaving any minute—if indeed it had not already left. Wally glanced swiftly at the kitchen clock.

"It's nine o'clock now," he said, "an' they've got to join the *Alabama* at Birkenhead before she moves into the Mersey to catch the second tide, which is at twelve thirty. It's a three-hour journey from here to Liverpool, so they'll only just make it. And if we're goin' to travel along with 'em, we'd better look slippy!"

"Travel *with* them?" cried Raymond and Laura at once. "How can we do that?"

"Follow me an' you'll see," said Wally, disappearing through the door after the impatient Mullinger, "an' you'd better come along too, Constable," he shouted back as he ran. "There may be some arrestin' to do before today's over."

After four or five minutes of breathless running through the twisting side streets of the town, Raymond was surprised to find that Wally (who for once had kept in the lead with Mullinger) was not heading for the railway sidings behind Central Station. Instead, he was heading away from the town center and toward Castleworth Bridge, where the railway passed out from the central industrial area and moved toward the suburbs and the country beyond. Raymond knew the bridge well because it used to be one of his favorite places for train spotting, and as they ran onto it now, his nostrils caught the acrid smell of steam trains, so much more thrilling and exciting to him than the diesels that he saw most of the time.

From the bridge, which was a triple-arched stone structure

about forty feet above the rails, you could see right up and down the lines in both directions: downward, they fanned out like the strands of a spider's web toward Manchester and the south, while upward they rushed together in a complicated labyrinth of switches and crossings leading to the platforms of Central Station and the freight yards beyond. It was toward these freight yards that Wally was now anxiously gazing, and sure enough after a few seconds a black engine pulling six cars and a caboose moved slowly out and came toward the bridge with gathering speed. Even from a distance Raymond easily recognized it as *No. 336 Vulcan,* and for a moment he forgot all about the dangerous adventure he was embarked upon and just wished that he had remembered to bring his notebook with him so that he could put another cross against *Vulcan* to indicate a second spotting. Then he saw that Wally had clambered onto the parapet of the bridge, and his heart stood still with fear.

Wally looked back at Laura and Raymond, and at P. C. Crumble, who had just come puffing up to join them. Seeing Raymond's anxious face, Wally grinned and pointed to the signal controlling the track that *Vulcan* was taking toward the bridge.

"What does the signal tell us, Raymond?"

Raymond studied it for a moment. It was the old-fashioned semaphore type of signal, set upward at an angle halfway between vertical and horizontal.

"It means 'Caution,' " he said at last.

"Exactly!" said Wally. "And 'Caution' near a crowded junction like this means ten miles an hour or even less. That's just a nice speed for us to drop down into the last two cars as they go under. Raymond and Laura jump first when I give the word. Me an' Mullinger an' the constable will follow. The cars is full of cotton waste covered with tarpaulin, so you'll 'ave a nice soft landin'."

In spite of Wally's reassuring words, Raymond was filled with horror as his eye measured the distance from the parapet of the bridge to the line below. He had never learned to dive at school, but once, dared by a friend, he had climbed up to the top board and crept along to the end, intending to jump off. But when he saw the greenish-blue water so far below, he had been terrified at the idea of letting his body plummet down into it from such a height, and so he had crept back down again while everybody laughed and jeered. But now this bridge was higher than that board, and he was going to have to jump, not into six and a half feet of clear still water, but into a clanking railway car of wood and iron, moving away from him at ten miles an hour, so that if he mistimed his jump even by a few seconds his body would be broken on the huge couplings and then mangled to bits beneath the relentless wheels.

But there was no help for it, and it was better to be crushed to death on the line than not to take the terrifying leap that would bring him close to Mr. Hamilton. So, pressing Laura's hand to give her courage, he climbed up on the parapet, where they stood together as the black train slowly rumbled toward them.

As the engine passed under the bridge, its funnel emitted a sudden whoosh of thick yellowish-black vapor, which blundered upward and enveloped them in a dense cloud. Raymond had kept his eye firmly fixed on the fifth car, but now he could see nothing, and he knew that he would have to jump blind, relying on Wally's judgment for a safe landing. But he had hardly had time to let this terrible thought sink in when Wally uttered his word of command, and, with a final squeeze of Laura's hand, he stepped off the parapet into the swirling cloud of steam and smoke.

Down, down, down he dropped, not like a stone, not like a dead weight, but like a sack of sand in which every grain ached with a fear that was worse than any sickness he had ever known. Then, *ker-plunk!* he landed, miraculously still on his feet, on a soft, springy tarpaulin, and instinctively bent his knees and went into a forward roll as he had seen parachutists do on television.

Laura landed beside him in a heap of soft fluffy cotton waste, and they lay there for what seemed like an endless moment, clinging to each other so tightly that they thought their arms would crack and their hearts would burst for joy.

Then a furry body flopped and floundered with them among the cotton waste, a warm wet tongue began to lick their faces, and opening their eyes they saw Mullinger smiling his biggest smile and Wally's twinkly face peering at them over the rim of the next car. It was only after another joyful bout of hugs and licks and kisses that a new fear suddenly gripped Raymond's heart, and looking up at Wally he asked in a small, tight voice:

"Where's Constable Crumble?"

Wally's eyes twinkled even more as he pointed back toward the bridge. The constable was beginning to heave himself slowly and ponderously up onto the parapet just as a second and longer train loaded with fresh clay was passing under the arch. The constable peered down at it doubtfully for a moment, apparently unable to make up his mind whether this was the right train or not, but then, as the last car but one began to slide under, he stood stiffly to attention, adjusted his tunic and took one step forward, landing with perfect timing amid the squelchy contents of the final car.

Once clear of the town, *Vulcan* gathered speed and was soon hurtling at sixty miles an hour alongside that very same canal where Raymond and Laura had drifted or plodded so slowly the day before. The engine was blowing off at full pressure, and its cars were clanking and swaying alarmingly on the bends and downward gradients. Raymond could tell that the driver was driving recklessly in his race against time, because he ignored the speed warnings posted at some parts of the track, and he didn't stop at the beginning of steep descents to pin down the brakes on the cars, but relied entirely on the engine brakes to check the speed.

Even so, Raymond was enjoying the ride, and as he clung to Laura he had that same feeling of terror mixed with excitement that he had had once at the fair when his mother had taken him on the Big Dipper. They flashed through the country stations and wayside halts with the arrogance of an express, leaving sleepy porters scratching their heads in bewilderment, and bearded, top-hatted station masters thumbing anxiously through timetables to find out if there was a new Blackstone-Liverpool nonstop service they hadn't noticed before. But as they approached Manchester the driver brought the train more under control, and it was now possible for Wally to make himself heard above the noise of the clattering cars and the hooting engine.

"It'll be time to take over as soon as we get to t'other side o' Manchester."

Raymond and Laura looked at him blankly. "Did you say . . . 'take over'?" said Raymond, feeling sure that he hadn't heard right.

"Yes," replied Wally cheerfully. "What you don't know about engine driving I probably do, and between us we're bound to make a better job of it than the crazy pair who're in the cab now. By the way, do you prefer to be engineer or fireman?"

Raymond's eyes sparkled. He could hardly believe that he was actually being offered a chance to drive a locomotive. Only once in his life had he ever been in the cab, and that was when a friendly engineer, whom he used to wave to from Castleforth Bridge, had invited him to spend a day in the switching yards. Now here was a chance to show what he had learned.

"I'll drive first," he said eagerly. "After that we can take turns if you like."

It was Laura who brought him down to earth with a bump.

"Raymond," she said, squeezing his hand kindly, "Wally's only joking. The three of us are no match for two grown men—even with Mullinger's help," she added, giving Mullinger a tickle behind the ears.

Wally struck his forehead in mock surprise. " 'Ow silly of me!" he said, with a more than usually mischievous grin. "I forgot to mention that I've brought a few reserves along."

He raised his trumpet, and—pitching the sound high and clear but not so loud as to reach to the engineer's cab or penetrate the grim thick boards of the caboose—he blew the brisk lively notes of reveille. At once, out of the other four tarpaulin-covered cars, heads began to appear—dozens of heads, scores of heads—heads of leggers, heads of sleepers-out, heads of climbing boys, heads of every size and shape and sort and color of boy that Raymond and Laura had ever seen or could ever imagine in Wally's motley collection. All were tousled, all were grubby, but all were bright-eyed and pink-cheeked, and as they stood up or squatted on the tops of the tarpaulins, Raymond noticed that they all had strong, sturdy limbs and tough, healthy little bodies.

The train was now coming into the gloomy smoke-blackened outskirts of Manchester, and Wally signaled to the boys to take cover again until they got clear of the city. So one by one the heads disappeared, and as the train rumbled through the central stations and freight yards, Wally outlined his plan to the children.

"About three miles out 'o Manchester, there's a very nasty curve at the top of a steep gradient. On that bend they'll 'ave to slow down to practically walkin' pace, and that'll be our chance. The boys'll 'op out when I give the signal, an' they'll 'ave that engineer an' fireman trussed up like Christmas turkeys in next to no time. Then we'll take the train on to Liverpool, an' there'll be a nice welcome for Mr. 'Amilton—an' a very *different* sort o' welcome for Mr. 'Arper—when we arrive."

Raymond and Laura clapped with delight at this prospect, but as the mill chimneys of Manchester began to recede into the background and the train started to breathe more heavily as it chugged up the first stretch of steep wooded hill, a shadow of anxiety came into their faces. Perhaps the engineer and the fireman were armed. Certainly they would be reckless and brutal men, since they were in the pay of Harper and Grimskull. And might not Harper himself begin to get suspicious when the train slowed down and come out of the caboose to investigate? But there was no point in dwelling on these fears, for already the sharp curve on the top edge of the steep hillside had come into view, and Wally was standing up to sound the charge.

The tousled heads reappeared, and the boys tumbled out of the cars on each side of the line. At the head of one column was

Sam Clegg, and at the head of the other was Nick, the oldest of the climbing boys. A few other boys, led by Tim and Paddy, wriggled forward like Apaches over the edge of the front cars and onto the tender, until they were crouching, ready to spring, directly behind the driver and fireman. At a second signal from Wally, they pounced, and while the amazed engineer and fireman struggled to release themselves from this grip, they were attacked by another crowd from below—namely Sam, Nick, and Co., who swarmed into the cab and swept the engineers off into the ditch, where Wally quickly secured their hands and feet in what he called his inescapable knot.

It was all over in a few seconds, but during those few seconds the train slowly ground to a halt, and had not Raymond reached the brake handle in time, it would have begun to roll back. He opened the blower valve, and an immediate screech of escaping steam told him that there was plenty of pressure to drive the pistons, but still he ordered Wally to keep stoking the blazing fire hole because he knew he would need all the pressure he could raise to get the train moving again on a steep grade like this.

After a few minutes of furious stoking, the pressure gauge rose to maximum, and Raymond cautiously released the brake and opened the regulator. He felt the engine take the strain of the heavy cars behind as if it were about to move slowly forward against the enormous down drag of the hill. But it was stuck, and though he gradually opened the regulator to near maximum, he could get no further pull on the train.

For a moment he felt completely baffled, and a sense of embarrassed failure came over him, such as he had sometimes felt at school when caught by the teacher on something he should have known. Wally was still stoking like mad, looking like a little red gnome in the fierce glow of the firebox, and Laura was standing timidly by, with a look of anxious concern on her face. It was that look of anxiety that tormented Raymond most of all: Laura *trusted* him to bring them through safely, and he had almost boasted to her and Wally that he could handle the controls and get the train moving. But now here he was, stuck like a dunce in a corner, without a single idea in his head.

But wait a moment—that very word "corner" gave him an idea! He suddenly remembered that on a sharp corner or curve it was often difficult to start a locomotive because the wheels tended to slip on the rails, especially if the rails were wet. They surely were wet on this section of the track, which was overhung by dripping trees and sheltered all the time from the sun. Should he increase the pressure or lower it? Or should he let the train roll back to a straighter and drier section of the line before attempting to restart?

He was feverishly trying to decide when the wheels suddenly gripped of their own accord, and the engine leaped forward, rounded the curve at the top of the gradient, and began the steep descent on the other side.

But even before Laura's scream pierced his ears, he knew that a terrible thing had happened: the wheel slip had set up shuddering vibrations in the leading car, and the strain of the powerful engine's sudden lurch forward had snapped the already weakened couplings. The train had split in two, and the engine was rushing headlong down one side of the hill while the cars and caboose were rolling back out of control down the other!

Wally glanced up from his stoking and read the message of alarm on Raymond's face. He turned from the fire hole and crossed over to the engineer's side of the cab, where Raymond and Laura were standing. It was lucky that he did so, because at that moment a huge sheet of flame leaped from the overstoked furnace.

It was a blowback! Had Wally been standing in his earlier position he would have been burned to a cinder. As it was, both he and the children were scorched by the blast, and the ominous smell of singed hair and clothing pervaded the cabin. Then the tongue of flame receded and Wally kicked the fire door shut, but a heap of oily rags and greasy boiler suits had caught fire, and the cabin was ablaze.

Mullinger had already leaped back onto the tender when the

blowback first occurred, but for Wally and the children this was impossible now that the cab itself had become an inferno. All they could do was climb down onto the iron steps at the side of the engine, and there cling for dear life to the brass handles. Here, as the engine increased speed, they were nearly swept off by the force of the rushing wind, and it was only the strength of Wally's tough little arms and the powerful grip of his short stubby fingers that enabled the children to hang on. And yet they would almost rather have flung themselves off to escape those terrible flames, which, fanned by the wind in the open cab, kept darting out at their faces and licking down toward their stretched and straining fingers!

Just when Raymond felt that he would pass out if he had to stand another instant of this agonizing ordeal by wind and speed and fire, he sensed that the train was slowing down a little and that more smoke than flame was coming from the cab—a filthy, choking, oily smoke certainly, but more bearable than the terrifying heat that had produced it. Little by little, too, the track leveled out, and when he ventured to open his tightly screwed-up eyes, Raymond saw that the engine was now running along an embankment built across a huge, dead-flat plain. Clambering back warily and painfully into the smoke-filled cab, he groped for the regulator and jammed it shut. Gradually the engine lost momentum and came to a halt.

Apart from the angry hissing of the boiler, there was silence over the whole plain. Wally and the children scrambled down to the side of the embankment and lay there exhausted, breathing in the cool fresh air and feeling the comfort of the firm sun-warmed earth against their bodies. Mullinger jumped down from the tender and fussed around them, gently licking their blistered hands and fanning their scorched faces with his tail.

For a long time Raymond lay there completely numb, unable to think or feel anything. Then gradually, painfully, thoughts and sensations began to return, but they were thoughts of despair and sensations of hopeless misery. How terribly he had failed! How stupid he had been not to realize about the wheel

slip in time to take the proper measures! How foolish he had
been to give Wally the wrong instructions about stoking the
firebox! If only he hadn't tried to show off by insisting on being
the first to drive, everything would have been all right! But now
everything was wrong. Mr. Hamilton and the boys were probably dead—derailed in their headlong rush down that terrible
slope. Wally would never trust him again—and Laura . . . Laura
must hate him!

But, no . . . Laura didn't hate him. As he gazed desolately up
at the sky through tears of grief and shame, Laura leaned over
and kissed him gently on the lips. At the same time he felt
Wally's knobbly hand giving his own hand a squeeze—and
Mullinger conferred on him the greatest of all canine compli-
ments by planting his bottom fairly and squarely on his chest!

Not a word was spoken, but Raymond knew that he was
forgiven, and that his friends loved him even more after his silly
mistakes than they did before them. Edging Mullinger gently
into a more convenient position, he sat up and gazed around. It
was certainly a barren and deserted scene. On all sides, as far as
the eye could see, there stretched away a flat peat bog, on which
the only vegetation was an occasional clump of rushes, hinting
at the slimy depths into which an unwary traveler could so
easily be sucked.

And suddenly it dawned on Raymond where he was. This
must be the famous Chat Moss, a huge peat bog, where, when he
built the Manchester–Liverpool Railway, George Stephenson
had done something which all the world had said was impossible. He had laid the track straight across the treacherous marsh
by floating it on a kind of raft made of woven bracken and
heather; on top of this he piled the stony ballast on which to
build up embankments and lay sleepers. For many weary
months hundreds of thousands of tons of earth and rubble,
which Stephenson poured into the marsh, had just sunk away
out of sight, swallowed up, everybody had said, by a bog which
no man would ever be able to reclaim. But at length the raft had
begun to hold, and a firm track emerged, which would carry

even the huge high-speed locomotives of the twentieth century across its springy bed of peat.

Suddenly Wally sat up and said: "Well, now, are we all fit to go on?"

"But . . . " said Laura and Raymond both together.

"But what?" said Wally. "If you're goin' to say, "But what about Mr. 'Amilton,' well, I've a feeling 'e'll come through safe an' sound, and in any case 'e wouldn't want us to dilly-dally while the *Alabama* slips away. An' if you're goin' to say, 'It's too late to stop the *Alabama*,' well, you may be right, but it's a flat run from 'ere to Liverpool an' Raymond know 'ow to get a nice turn o' speed out of this old *Vulcan*."

"Do you mean that . . . you want me to drive?" said Raymond incredulously.

"Of course, who else?" said Wally, climbing up into the cab and seizing the stoking shovel.

So once again Raymond found himself up in the cab, checking the gauges and anxiously testing the pressure. Laura found a brush in the toolbox at the front of the tender, so she swept out all the charred bits of clothing and then brought a canful of water from the water-storage compartment so that they could all cool their parched faces and lips. It took about ten minutes to raise enough steam to get moving, but eventually *Vulcan* responded to Wally's energetic stoking and Raymond's careful manipulation of valves and regulator. Grumpily at first, but with increasing willingness, it chuffed away down the long straight line.

Sometimes they passed other trains going in the opposite direction, and then Raymond let Laura sound off the whistle in greeting, while he waved at the astonished crew of the passing train or gave them a smart salute to the visor of his engineer's cap. Once, as a slow freight train rumbled by, the children could see that the cars were filled with sacks of American grain that had been sent over by the merchants of the Northern states to help feed the hungry workers of the Lancashire towns. But, alas, none of the trains were carrying cotton, which was the real food of those towns.

It was not until they had crossed Chat Moss and got beyond Kenyon Junction that any train came up from behind them. But then they became aware of a powerful freight engine gradually drawing abreast of them, for a moment giving them the funny impression that they were themselves moving backward. Raymond recognized it as a Yates 0-6-0 type, and was so busy looking for its name and number (it was called *No. 707 Conqueror*) that at first he didn't notice a strange figure signaling frantically to him from the opposite cab.

It was Constable Crumble—but how different from the spruce blue-uniformed figure with which they were so familiar. *This* Constable Crumble was not a bit spruce—he was soiled and splattered and bedraggled. He was not blue-uniformed either—he was brown-uniformed and brown-faced too, for that matter, and he looked more like a chocolate soldier than a police constable. From the soles of his colossal boots to the tip of his tall helmet he was covered in clay, which the heat from the firebox had baked into a hard crust. Bits of clay flaked off him as he waved, and his face, as he desperately tried to shout something above the din of the two engines, was cracked and cratered like a photograph of the moon.

But what was it that he was trying to shout? And how did he come to be up in the cab of the train when he had started off in the rear car? Neither Raymond nor Laura nor Wally could frame an answer to these puzzling questions, and if Mullinger knew one, he didn't say. It almost seemed as if the constable's main object was to challenge them to a race, because he seemed to be waving Raymond back and urging his own engineer to go faster. Wally and Raymond took up the challenge, but slowly the more powerful engine drew ahead in spite of its heavier load, and *Vulcan's* crew found themselves gazing into car after car of thick brown clay.

Then, as the last clay car drew ahead (they could tell it was the last because it still bore in it the perfect imprint of a large policeman), they saw to their amazement that there were other cars behind, and that these cars were filled with cheering, waving boys, and that behind these cars full of boys was the grim black caboose with its stout heavy timbers and small iron grilles. This, then, was what P. C. Crumble had been trying to show them, but they had been so intent upon urging *Vulcan* forward that they had never thought of glancing back!

How their hearts jumped for joy at the sight of the merry faces of the boys—and even more at the sight of the caboose, black and forbidding though it was! Good old Crumble! Somehow or other he had had the presence of mind to check the runaway train and to get it coupled up to his own train. How they blessed him for his stupidity now that his blunder at the bridge had turned out to have had such a happy result!

As they approached the Sankey Viaduct, which carries the track over the canal at a height of seventy feet, *No. 707 Conqueror* began to lose speed, and Raymond realized that this was probably due to overstoking, which often smothers the fire and makes the engine sluggish. Now was his chance to overtake, so, with Wally stoking at just the right level, he slowly built up pressure and pulled ahead. *Vulcan* was first across the viaduct, but *Conqueror* was not far behind; and at the Rainhill Level, where Stephenson's *Rocket* had raced against its rivals way back in the earliest days of the railway, the two engines were neck and neck. So they raced on, fighting every inch of the way, through the deep rock cutting at Olive Mount and the long tunnel at Edgehill, until the cranes and masts of the Liverpool and Birkenhead shipyards came into sight, and they knew that their journey was nearly over.

The switches were set for both trains to branch off to the Birkenhead yards, but it was *Vulcan* which was first to come to rest with a clank and a jolt against the terminal buffers. *No. 707 Conqueror* drew up alongside just a few seconds later. The time by the clock on the dockyard tower was twelve noon.

The first thing Laura and Raymond did was to jump out and give the clay-caked Crumble a big hug and a kiss. Then, without giving him a chance to put this irregular event down in his notebook, they dragged him along to the end of the train, followed eagerly by Wally, Mullinger, and all the boys. The caboose was still locked and silent. Laura hammered on the thick door and shouted through the grille:

"Papa, it's Laura. Wally's here, too, and Raymond, and we have a policeman and lots of boys to help us. You needn't fear any harm from Harper now. We've got the caboose surrounded."

There was still silence inside except for one slight noise which made Laura and Raymond turn pale. It was the sound of a pistol being cocked. Wally looked down at his boots, studying them intently. Mullinger raised one paw and looked up at him with his head on one side as if to ask, "What would you like me to do?" P. C. Crumble reached for his truncheon. Then Harper's harsh American voice came through, mocking and confident as ever:

"It wouldn't make any difference, girlie, if you had the whole of the British Army out there—let alone a pack of kids and a stupid policeman. Because I've got your pop in here as my hostage, and I swear to God I'll put a bullet through his brain if you don't let me through to the *Alabama*. You've got five minutes to decide. After that it'll be too late."

Raymond and Laura looked at each other in consternation. They had never thought of this possibility. Wally was still studying his boots. Mullinger was pawing the ground impatiently. Then another voice spoke from the van—a calm, clear voice that made Raymond feel safe and secure in spite of the terrible dangers that threatened.

"Listen to me carefully, Laura," said the voice. "Take no notice of this man's threats. He's bluffing. He won't dare to harm me. And in any case what happens to me is not important. I am fighting a battle against the evils of slavery, and you and Raymond and Wally and the boys are all fighting with me. If we die in battle, we die well, and our deaths will help the Cause. There is still time to stop the *Alabama*. Go quickly with the constable and alert the dockyard police. They have a warrant to prevent her sailing."

Laura looked questioningly at Wally, and Wally nodded to her to obey. So, taking Mullinger and the constable and a handful of the boys, she dashed away across the cobbles and railway lines in quest of the dockyard offices. Then Wally turned to Raymond and whispered:

"Quickly now. Everhthing depends on you. I'll stay 'ere and keep 'Arper talkin' for a few more minutes. Then I'll 'ave to let 'im out. The *Alabama* was built across the river in Birkenhead, but she's been moved here to Liverpool and is now berthed at Number Twelve Wharf. You get over there with some of the boys and ambush 'Arper as 'e comes along to the quayside. There'll be plenty of 'idin' places an' 'e won't be expectin' you. But be careful—'e'll shoot."

Raymond nodded and looked at the boys. Dozens of eager faces crowded around him, all wanting to be included in the mission. At school he had never enjoyed being chosen to pick a team because he never liked leaving anybody out. But now he knew he had to pick his team quickly and carefully, because too many would spoil the operation, and he had to have just the right ones.

"I'll take Nick, Tim, Paddy, Chris, and Tom," he said decisively; and then, when the rest continued to look pleadingly at him, he added Sam Clegg to the list and the four leggers who had pushed Kieran's barge through the tunnel.

"That's enough now," he said, and set off at once toward the looming masts and funnels of the quayside.

As they dashed along, following the huge numbered signs that indicated the different sections of the shipbuilding yards, Raymond marveled at the size and variety of the ships under construction all around him. Massive steamers were being built alongside graceful seven-masted schooners, and between these two extremes there was every combination of sail and steam imaginable. There was a three-master with a wooden hull and one funnel, driven by a paddlewheel set amidships; and there was an iron warship with turret guns, driven by a huge propeller at the stern. Some of the ships must have looked old-fashioned even as they were being built, and others would still not look too out of date if they were steaming out of the Mersey today.

How strange it was, thought Raymond, that a hundred years ago everything was so different and so similar. Perhaps time was only a sort of optical illusion after all. He had always imagined that past ages were dim and distant and remote, but now he felt that they were just as real as the present—in fact they *were* the present, somehow, and everything that had happened in history was happening all the time, forever.

By now they had reached No. 9 Wharf . . . then No. 10 . . . No. 11 . . . and finally, between two tall warehouses, they spotted the sign for No. 12. Here Raymond slowed down and ordered the boys to follow him in single file through the dark narrow alley that led onto the wharf. Obediently they dropped back, and Raymond advanced cautiously into the entry, noting as he went that the warehouses had loading bays at intervals, about twelve feet from the ground, and that from some of the bays protruded the long arms of mechanical hoists. He also noted, with relief, that there were hardly any shipyard workers to be seen. It was twelve noon, and most of them would have knocked off for their midday break. So, beckoning the boys forward, he crept around the corner and onto the wharf.

What he saw there took his breath away with amazement. It was a long, slender, black-hulled ship carrying three sharply raked masts and a tall central funnel for her steam engines. There were no cannon aboard her that Raymond could see, but several devices along her sides appeared suspiciously like gun mounts. She looked light, fast, and dangerous, and Raymond could easily picture her in his mind's eye, streaking through the gray Atlantic waves and blasting other vessels out of the water before they even knew she was near.

This, then, was the engine of destruction built by the wealth of the cotton lords and the sufferings of their slaves. This was the vessel that was to wreak havoc upon the shipping of the Northern states. Already her crew were loosening the hawsers and standing by to take up the gangplank, and one of them, slung in a basket from the rounded stern, was just completing the painting of her name, *Alabama*, in place of the shipyard number—666—under which her identity had been concealed during the many months of building.

But there was no more time to stand and gaze. A low whistle from Sam Clegg, who had stayed behind at the other end of the alley to act as lookout, warned Raymond that Harper was approaching with his hostage. Quickly the ambushers positioned themselves in accordance with Raymond's orders in the part of the alley over which the looming warehouses cast their darkest shadows. The climbing boys shinned up to the loading bays and wriggled out along the arms of the hoists, Nick, Tim, and Paddy on one arm, and Chris and Tommy on another. Sam Clegg crept behind a refuse bin, and the leggers melted away into a dark and cavernous porch. Casting a final look around to make quite sure that they were all invisible, Raymond caught hold of the dangling end of a block and tackle, which was suspended from a beam across the alley, and clambered with it up an iron waterspout, ready to swing out on it as he had seen boys do on the ropes in the school gym.

He was not a moment too soon. Footsteps approached the alley, and Raymond saw the tall stately figure of Mr. Hamilton rounding the corner, wrists bound but head erect, closely guarded by Harper, whose pistol was pressed to his captive's temple. Wally and the rest of the boys followed some distance behind, afraid to intervene in case Harper pulled the trigger.

Raymond waited until Harper had passed him and was almost under the arms of the hoists. Then he launched himself silently through the air on the block and tackle and landed with his legs around Harper's neck, exactly as Wally had done in the drive on Grimskull Lodge. At the same moment, the climbing boys dropped from the hoists, and Sam and the leggers hurled themselves from the shadows.

Harper staggered under the onslaught, but he was a huge, powerful man and he managed to stay on his feet. Kicking and cursing like a maniac, he flung the boys from him in all directions, then whirled around in fury to aim his pistol point-blank at Mr. Hamilton's face. Raymond, who had been hurled like a rag doll from his brawny shoulders, leaped up and dragged his arm down, but the pistol went off and Mr. Hamilton fell to the ground, with a red stain appearing upon the frills of his immaculate white shirtfront.

At that very moment there was a blast from the *Alabama's* siren, announcing her imminent departure. Harper flung down the pistol and raced along the alley, with Raymond still clinging like grim death to the sleeve of his coat! The ship's gangplank had been withdrawn but had not yet been hauled aboard, and with a desperate leap Harper attempted to span the widening gap between it and the jetty. But the distance was too great, and he plunged headlong into the water, dragging Raymond with him.

Raymond could swim, but not well. He let go of Harper, rose to the surface, and struck out for the side, realizing that at any moment he might be drawn into the great churning propeller. But he had only made one stroke when he felt his legs clutched from below and he was dragged down, down, down to the very bottom of the basin. As they sank, Harper's legs flailed uselessly, and he clawed at Raymond's clothes and hair. Suddenly, with a mixture of wild hope and terrible fear, Raymond realized that *Harper could not swim.*

Slowly they rolled and wrestled to the bottom, and Harper's clutchings became more and more frantic as the oily water gushed into his lungs. Raymond held on as long as possible to the breath he had snatched on the surface, but at length it was all used up, and he too began to gulp and choke. A loud noise was drumming in his head, and it seemed as if his temples would burst. Then, just as he felt that the next moment his whole body would split open with the agonizing pressure, he became dimly aware of other swimming figures all around him, the figures of boys darting around like shoals of little fish, and he was tugged slowly upward from those hideous depths, upward to the air and light.

His head broke the surface, and he was hauled to the jetty by many willing hands. There he lay gasping and belching while P. C. Crumble gently but firmly pressed the water from his lungs. Then, while the constable reluctantly went to work on the unconscious Harper, he sat up and looked around him. The jetty was filled with boys and shipyard workers and dockyard police. But where were Laura and Mr. Hamilton? And what had happened to the *Alabama?* These questions swarmed in his head, so that he became giddy and felt himself keeling over. Then, just before he fainted, he knew the answers, for he caught sight of Laura's tear-stained face as she knelt beside the prostrate body of her father, and he heard the note of Wally's trumpet, strangely defiant in defeat, sounding from the end of the jetty where he stood watching the *Alabama* turn out and disappear into the open river.

9

NOT A PARTING
BUT A PARTY

*in which everyone takes part in a triumphal proces-
sion, and a party is held to celebrate a particularly
fortunate and felicitous turn of events.*

The first thing that Raymond noticed when he woke up was that
the hole in the wall had been temporarily boarded up. That was
a pity, because he'd been half hoping that he might persuade his
mother to come through with him to Mrs. Porson's kitchen, so
that she'd be able to see for herself that his friends on the other
side were real. The next thing he noticed was that the room
seemed very dark, and when he glanced up at the basement
window, he could see why. A large Pickford van had drawn up
outside, blocking out the light. He could see the legs of the driver
and his helper as they loaded articles of furniture from the
pavement into the van. As he saw the familiar objects—his
workbench, his train set, the two old fireside chairs—lying out
there in the street and being handled by strangers, he had an
odd sensation that his life didn't belong to him anymore. He
glanced around the room, which was hardly recognizable now
that it was nearly stripped. Only the old kitchen screen, which
had been in the flat since long before Raymond and his mother
had come to live there, was still standing in its accustomed
place, with its faded and mysterious picture of "Love and
Death," painted long ago by a Victorian artist called G. F.
Watts. There were white patches on the walls where other
pictures and calendars had been taken down, and the carpet was

quite threadbare where the chairs and sofa had been. He felt suddenly frightened in this unfamiliar room, and longed to be surrounded again with all the things he had got so used to seeing and touching during the nine and a half years of his life. Even the smell of the room was different now: it was musty somehow—almost moldy. To his horror he saw a beetle scuttle out of a crack that had been hidden by the cupboard, and there was a large spider's web in the corner of the window frame where the valance had hung.

But worse than this feeling of strangeness and loneliness, and worse than the fire that seemed to be raging in his fevered limbs was the sense of failure and defeat in his heart. He could remember nothing of the journey back from Liverpool, but he remembered only too clearly Laura's grief-stricken face and Mr. Hamilton's bloodstained body. He remembered too the glimpse he had had of the *Alabama* proudly pointing her nose toward the open sea. He had always felt sure that Mr. Hamilton would be saved and the *Alabama* prevented from sailing, but now all his hopes had been dashed and his dreams had turned into nightmares. A thought came into his head that was so terrible and startling that he found himself saying it out loud:

"Perhaps, after all, evil is stronger than good, and greedy and selfish people will always defeat the kind and generous ones."

"That's how it looks a lot of the time," said a voice, and turning around, Raymond discovered that Ben Oddy had been sitting all the time in the dark corner by his bed.

"So storybooks are all wrong then," said Raymond, "because in stories the goodies always win in the end, but it's not like that in real life, is it?"

"No," said Ben, "it's not. But the stories are still true, for all that."

"How can they be true if they're not like real life?"

"They *come* true if you believe them," said Ben, "but usually in ways you don't expect."

Raymond pondered this for a moment. He wasn't sure that he knew what Ben was driving at, but he was too tired to argue. In any case he didn't feel like arguing with Ben. Just talking to him and listening to his humorous drawling voice made him feel better.

"Thanks for the record," he said. "It was super."

"Glad you liked it," said Ben. "You didn't think it was too highbrow, then?"

"What's 'highbrow'?"

"Highbrow? Oh, it means, sort of, 'difficult to enjoy.' "

"Nothing's difficult to *enjoy*!" Raymond laughed.

It was Ben's turn to ponder. "I suppose you're right there," he said at length. "Children know more than grown-ups about enjoying things."

Just then the room got suddenly lighter as the Pickford van pulled away. Raymond looked up in alarm.

"They've forgotten my bed."

"Oh, they'll call back for it later," said Ben. "In any case you won't be needing it for a bit."

"Why not?"

"Because you're due for a spell in the hospital."

Raymond went very quiet. Then he asked, in a small, shriveled sort of voice: "What's it like in the hospital?"

"Nasty," said Ben.

"How nasty?"

"Oh, you know, pretty nurses fluffing your pillow up all the time. Lots of fruit, new toys, and visitors."

Raymond smiled, but he still looked anxious about something. After a moment or two he asked: "Will I be able to have . . . *any* kind of visitors?"

"Like who, for instance?"

"Well, like . . . Wally."

Ben grinned his lazy grin. "*He* won't need to visit you. He works there!"

"But . . . I thought he was a chimney sweep, busker, and escape artist."

"So he is, but he's also a part-time ambulance driver, ward orderly, and hospital porter."

That was certainly good news, but Raymond's head was throbbing so badly that he had to lie back. Then Ben started humming a song Raymond half recognized as another of Mr. Jeffars' specials:

> Good news, chariot's a-comin', good news,
> Chariot's a-comin', good news,
> An' I don't want it to leave a-me behind.

Raymond was thrilled by the lively, lilting melody. He forgot his headache and joined in the next verse with a clear, steady voice:

> There'll be peace an' freedom in this world, I know,
> Peace an' freedom in this world, I know,
> An' I don't want it to leave a-me behind.

As the chorus "Good news" began again, it was taken up by the familiar note of a trumpet, and Wally appeared at the door in the uniform of an ambulance driver.

Folding up the old kitchen screen and using it as a stretcher, he and Ben hustled Raymond into the ambulance and drove away at top speed, flashing the emergency lights and sounding the siren.

Hee-ha hee-ha! went the siren as Wally turned into the main street and zoomed recklessly in and out of the traffic. Raymond held tightly on to Ben's hand to steady himself against the lurch and roll of the ambulance as it screeched around sharp corners or accelerated suddenly to beat the lights. Though he was feeling sick and desperately tired, he was excited by the speed and felt quite important at the thought of all the cars, buses, and trucks that were having to give way to him. Then, to his disappointment, he heard Wally changing down from top gear to third, then from third to second, and soon they were crawling along at a snail's pace in first.

"Drat it!" Wally shouted back from the driver's cab. "We've got stuck in some sort of demonstration."

Raymond struggled up painfully on one arm and peered through the one-way blue glass. The streets were full of people marching along in procession, shouting slogans and carrying banners and signs. Many of them were dark-skinned people—Africans and Pakistanis and Indians and West Indians—but many were also white, and on their signs were written slogans like "FAIR DEAL FOR IMMIGRANTS" and "NO SLAVERY HERE."

The police were accompanying the demonstrators along the route and breaking up the scuffles that developed when angry counterdemonstrators tried to intervene. One scuffle took place right outside the window of the ambulance, and with a sudden start, Raymond thought he heard a familiar voice saying, " 'Ello, 'ello, 'ello, wot's all this 'ere then?—and sure enough, a moment later, Constable Crumble appeared and took charge of the situation. But, no—it wasn't Constable Crumble anymore—it was *Sergeant* Crumble, with three large glossy new stripes on his arm to prove it!

But that was only the first of Raymond's surprises. As the demonstrators trooped by, he caught sight of a party of West Indians, laughing and joking and flashing their white teeth, but when he looked more closely at them, he realized that most of them were not West Indians at all, but climbing boys, with soot-blackened faces and merry mischievous eyes.

And to make matters more confusing still, the demonstration seemed to be turning into a carnival procession! People were dancing and singing and throwing streamers and climbing onto the tops of buses and cars, and many of them were wearing old-fashioned costumes—clogs and shawls and crinolines and frock coats and tall hats. And horse-drawn carriages mingled with motor vehicles, Volkswagens alongside hansom cabs, brewers' drays battling for position with tractor trailers.

Slowly the procession sorted itself out, and as it passed from the narrow streets of the town center and began to move up the wide highway that led to Moorland Hospital, Raymond could see that the whole town was streaming out in the same direction, and both sides of the road were filled with cheering, marching people.

By cheeky driving, Wally gradually wormed his way to the front of the procession, but he didn't rush right ahead—instead, he stayed just behind the leading cart, which was a huge mill wagon bearing the name "Charles Hamilton and Co. Ltd.," drawn by a magnificent white horse with flowing mane and tail, which Raymond recognized at once as Snowdrift. On the back of the cart the town band, resplendent in their braided uniforms, were pumping out a stirring march:

> "John Brown's body lies a-molderin' in the grave
> John Brown's body lies a-molderin' in the grave
> John Brown's body lies a-molderin' in the grave
> But his soul goes marchin' on!"

And behind them thousands of voices took up the chorus:

> "Glory glory alleluia
> Glory glory alleluia
> Glory glory alleluia
> And his soul goes marchin' on!"

So the procession wound its way out of the town, climbing gradually toward the edge of the moors, where a brand-new hospital had recently been erected on the site of an old mill owner's estate. Here Snowdrift turned into the hospital gates, and as the rest of the marchers swarmed through and spread out all over the hospital grounds like holiday picnickers, Wally drove the ambulance along a pleasant rhododendron-bordered drive and pulled up in front of one of the main wards.

"Terminal station!" shouted Ben Oddy, and before Raymond quite realized what was happening, he had been whisked out of the ambulance and found himself propped up on the pillows of a clean bed, with a pretty nurse bending over him.

The nurse wore a white starched cap and a long blue dress with starched collar and cuffs. As she bent closer to him, Raymond opened his mouth obediently, expecting the thermometer. Instead, she threw her arms around him and gave him a kiss.

It was Laura! For a few minutes she fussed around him, putting proper hospital corners on the bedclothes, arranging a few favorite toys and a giant bottle of lemonade on his nightstand, and wheeling a trolley table up across the bed, already set with plates and cutlery and napkins. There was even a wineglass too, Raymond noticed—so hospital meals must be very special indeed!

Then Laura sat down on the edge of the bed and held both his hands in hers.

"It'll be visiting time soon," she said, "but before they all come we can have a few minutes to ourselves. Today's a special day and there's going to be a party. Mrs. Porson's doing the cooking."

"What are we celebrating?"

"Oh, all sorts of things. To start with, Constable Crumble has been promoted to sergeant."

"Yes, I know," laughed Raymond. "I saw him on the way up. How on earth did he manage that?"

"He was promoted for saving the train and arresting Harper. But we get the reward because we gave the information leading to the arrest."

Raymond whistled. "Fifteen hundred dollars! We'll never manage to spend all that!"

"We don't have to spend it. It's much more fun to give it away."

"Who shall we give it to, though?"

"To Mrs. Porson, for a wedding present!"

"But," said Raymond, a horrible doubt beginning to fill his mind, "who is she going to marry?"

"Guess!"

"Wally—no, Crumble—no, Wally. Oh, I can't guess—you'll have to tell me."

"Well, it's Crumble. She says she still loves them both, but she's marrying Crumble to build up the forces of law and order for the sake of the British Empire."

"What does Wally think?"

"He's delighted. He says that even Houdini couldn't have pulled off such a tricky escape."

"So it's a promotion party, a reward party, and an engagement party! What else is it?"

"It's a get-well party."

"For me?"

"Yes, for you, and for Father."

Raymond looked at her incredulously. So many surprising things had happened today that he had begun to think that nothing could surprise him anymore. But this was fantastic. He had seen Mr. Hamilton with his own eyes—lying there, shot through the heart. He shuddered again at the thought of it and turned his face to the pillow.

"Raymond, look at me," said Laura, gently turning his face around with her hand. "You have to believe what I'm going to tell you. Then in a moment you'll see it for yourself. But you must promise to believe me first."

"All right, I promise," said Raymond. He knew, as he looked into those clear, candid eyes, that anything she told him must be true.

"You remember the brooch of hair that we made and put into the locket," said Laura. "And you remember how we threw the locket into the caboose with the ribbon, to tell Papa that we knew where he was and would come to save him. Well, he wore that locket next to his heart, and when you leaped at Harper and pulled the gun down, the bullet struck the locket and glanced off, missing his heart. It was a bad wound, but not a fatal one."

Raymond gazed at her in wonder and delight. Then he said thoughtfully:

"The hair—that's what saved him. I read somewhere that nothing is stronger than human hair."

"Nothing is stronger than human love," said a deep kindly

voice, and Raymond realized that as Laura had been telling her story Mr. Hamilton had glided up to the bedside in a wheelchair. And—here, for Raymond, came the biggest and best surprise of the whole day—the person pushing the wheelchair was a lady wearing a brand-new coat and hat and carrying a smart new shopping bag, whom it took him several moments to recognize as—his mother!

"Mummy," he cried, when she had finished hugging him, "how lovely you look—almost like a different person!"

"I *am* a different person," smiled Mrs. Price, and as she smiled Raymond noticed that the tense, anxious, careworn expression had gone from her face. "I've had a long talk with Mr. Hamilton, and I've met Wally and Mullinger and all your friends, and I don't feel at all worried about you anymore!"

"Oh," exclaimed Laura suddenly, "silly me! I've forgotten to let the visitors in, and they're all waiting at the end of the ward!"

She ran to the head nurse's office and tinkled a little bell, whereupon the visitors began to troop up the ward with their various offerings. Suddenly it seemed to Raymond that the drab ward was transformed into a scene of fun and gaiety—just like a huge Christmas party, with a Christmas tree and fairy lights, and Mr. Hamilton in the middle of it all, looking exactly like Father Christmas with his flowing beard.

In came the climbing boys, bringing a bag of chocolate mints (one or two of which had been licked on the way) and a copy of the latest issue of *The Railway Enthusiast*. Mullinger came next with something that might once have been a sausage roll, and he was followed by Wally, who brought *The Boys' Book of Great Escapes,* and Ben Oddy with *Music Star*. Wally had changed into his ward orderly's white coat, and Ben was wearing his clergyman's cassock with a leather belt, which Raymond thought he looked rather nice in.

Following them came Sergeant Crumble, with Mrs. Porson on his arm. The sergeant presented Raymond with a pair of toy handcuffs that were too big for his wrists and a policeman's helmet that was too small for his head, but they all had a laugh about this and the sergeant ended up wearing the tiny helmet as a party hat himself.

Then Sadie and Mary Ellen and Clara and Philomena and Lizzie, all dressed in neat black-and-white waitresses' outfits, wheeled in a string of trolleys groaning with chickens and hams and patties and pies and puddings and cakes and custards and creams such as Raymond had never set eyes on in his life before, and when they had all eaten as much as they could, Ben Oddy poured out the wine, raised his glass, and proposed a toast:

"To Mr. Hamilton, a dear father and a kind friend!"

Everybody drank to this, and then Wally jumped up and proposed: "To Mrs. Porson, for her beauty!"

This was followed by Raymond, who proposed: "To Sergeant Crumble, for his bravery!"

Other toasts followed thick and fast, and everybody got rather tipsy, including Mullinger, who drank a whole saucerful of wine at every toast. Then Wally picked up his trumpet to lead them off in a songfest, and they sang through every song in this book and many more besides, but by the time they got to the last one, Raymond, who of course was not used to drinking wine, was ready to doze off in Laura's arms, holding his mother's hand and gazing up contentedly at Mr. Hamilton's gently smiling face.

POSTSCRIPT

And what happened to the *Alabama?*

After her escape from Liverpool, she sailed to the Azores, where she was fitted out with guns, munitions, and crew, and then set out on her career as a commerce raider. And the C.S.S. *Alabama,* under the command of Captain Raphael Semmes of Mobile, was a brilliantly successful predator. Between July 29, 1862, when she slipped down the Mersey, and June 19, 1864, she burned, sank, or seized over eighty merchantmen—a record of devastation unequaled by any other single ship in naval history. She also sank one vessel of the U. S. Navy and outran or evaded several others. In fright, Northern shipowners began to change their vessels from American to British registry.

Lurid accounts of the *Alabama's* success were printed in English newspapers. Working people were horrified and held great mass meetings and street marches, demanding that their government should never again allow such a vessel to be built for the Confederates in a British port. Gradually, too, the rich merchants and cotton-mill owners realized that Mr. Hamilton had been right, and they too joined in the protest. When, a year after the *Alabama* had sailed, news came of twin Union victories at Gettysburg and Vicksburg, the government itself began to think that it had backed the wrong side. No more *Alabama*s were built, but a British vessel, the *Sea King,* was sold to Confederate agents in October, 1864, rechristened *Shenandoah,* and sent to the Bering Strait, where she decimated the United States whaling fleet.

The *Alabama* herself, worn out by her long cruise and short of coal, put in at the port of Cherbourg, France, in the middle of June, 1864. News of her arrival was telegraphed to Captain

John A. Winslow, skipper of the U.S.S. *Kearsarge,* then cruising off the coast of Holland. Winslow steamed to Cherbourg, lay off the harbor, and waited for the elusive raider to complete her repairs and emerge. There was plenty of warning that a sea battle was impending, so the enterprising French ran excursion trains from Paris, and as June 19 dawned, fifteen thousand spectators lined the Cherbourg cliffs, and a flotilla of pleasure boats followed the *Alabama* out of the harbor.

The show lasted an hour and ten minutes. The battling vessels were about the same size, but the light, swift *Alabama* was no match for her more heavily armored opponent. As they circled one another, three quarters of a mile apart, the *Kearsarge*'s gunners sent 11-inch shells accurately through her sides, one after another, until the Confederate flag came fluttering down. With the vessel sinking under them, the Southern crew abandoned ship. Semmes and his first lieutenant were picked up by the *Deerhound,* an English yacht whose owner had sailed out to watch the spectacle.

This was not quite the end of the *Alabama* story, however, for when the American Civil War was over, the United States pressed claims against Great Britain for damages caused by ships built by or bought from British subjects. In 1872 an international board of arbitration awarded the Americans $15.5 million in gold, and Great Britain paid it.

ABOUT THE AUTHOR

"Mullinger the dog," says author Colin Wood, "is a portrait of my own dog, Bob, who actually laughs. The story recalls memories of my own childhood in a Lancashire cotton town and deals indirectly with the illness of my little girl, who died in 1965."

A serious student of English literature, who concentrated on a study of Victorian social fiction, Mr. Wood is currently lecturer in English at All Saints College, Leeds, Yorkshire. He is married and the father of five children, and enjoys cycling, running, camping, tramping, and working with young people—a life he terms "outwardly uneventful."